The CUT BAIT MURDERS

A St. James City, Florida Mystery

BY MITCH GRANT

ISBN: 1495223930
ISBN 13: 9781495223938
Library of Congress Control Number: 2014904065
CreateSpace Independent Publishing Platform
North Charleston, South Carolina

This novel is dedicated to the residents of Pine Island and Saint James City who, unknowingly, have served as models for many of the "better-behaved" characters in this book. I would also like to thank them for being such genuinely nice people. In addition, I would like to thank the members of Pine Island Writers. Without their acceptance, support, feedback, and encouragement, this book would not have been possible. Finally, I want to thank my wife, Sherry, for understanding and tolerating the absences from the real world required for me to write yet another book.

Chapter One

Six months had passed since Carl Perez blew his brains out. Enough time for life on the island to have returned to normal... but it hadn't.

Saint James City, a quiet, remote fishing village, is located on the south end of Pine Island. Pine Island sits between the south-western Florida mainland and the sparkling beachfront barrier islands of Sanibel and Captiva. There are no beaches on Pine Island.

My name is Jim Story. My wife, Jill, and I retired to Saint James City last year. At that time life here had seemed almost magical. In some ways, it seemed almost as if time had managed to over-look our new quaint island home.

"Carefree" is the word that comes to mind when thinking back to those more pleasant days. Back then, everyone seemed happy, business was good for the few commercial establishments in town, and there was no crime. Old folks having health issues was the only trouble. But that seemed natural. Life here was good. Very good.

However, all of that seemed to change after Carl Perez killed my friend, Javier Hernandez. Somehow, it was almost as if that murder broke down the walls that had protected this isolated town from the realities of the modern world.

I guess the first weird thing that happened after the murder was when seventy-five-year-old Whitey Wiggs was killed as he was leaving Ragged Ass Saloon. The throttle on his ancient scooter stuck wide open, and he plowed into the hull of a sailboat that was sitting on stands, having its bottom painted at the marina across the street. Scratch one genuine island character.

The next tragedy was when Frank Albritton died. Frank was a good guy; He was retired, about seventy, living with his girlfriend in a house that backed up to a canal. He took their dog out for a walk one night. The dog came back, but Frank didn't. They searched all night but couldn't find him. Eventually, several days later, the authorities found his body. Apparently he'd had a heart attack and fallen into the canal. The tide had taken him toward the bay.

These somber events had cast a pall over the island. Still, as awful as they were, they could still be grouped together into the category of "that's life." Being killed in an accident and dropping dead from a heart attack—these things happen.

However, what was to come was anything but life as usual.

Chapter Two

Jill and I decided to have lunch in Matlacha. We were on our way into Cape Coma (the community otherwise known as Cape Coral) to tend to some required off-island shopping. We try to buy as much as we can on-island, but some things can only be reasonably sourced in "civilization." That's what we call the world that exists beyond the intersection of Pine Island Road and Burnt Store Road. Once you go through there, you're back in the real world, and all bets are off.

We pulled into the shell covered parking lot of Mulletville a little before noon. I love the name of this little restaurant. Mulletville was what they used to call the town of Matlacha before it acquired its current, more fashionable name. So, in some ways, the restaurant's moniker is a reminder of, and a throwback to, life in a different era. And so is the restaurant. It's plain. None of the tables, chairs, or booths really match, and the floor is bare concrete. All of that would be enough to turn off a lot of people, but it reminds me of some of the places I used to eat in Florida fifty years ago. I guess that's why I like it. That, and the food!

If I get there in time for breakfast, my favorite dish is mullet, eggs, and grits. Food doesn't get much better than that. But if I miss breakfast, as we did that day, I fall back on having a platter of fried mullet, coleslaw, and fries. That's genuine 'Florida Cracker' food, and it's hard to beat. I love it.

"Hi! Y'all come on in and take a seat—anywhere you like," was the friendly greeting we received as we came through the door. Nothing unusual about that. What was unusual was who had delivered the greeting. It took us both a couple of beats to get our arms around it. Jill, as usual, was quicker on the uptake than me.

"Jamie! I didn't expect to see you here. How are you?" Jill said.

"Oh, I'm doing great. Y'all get a good table by the windows, and I'll come by to check on you in a minute."

Jamie, good to her word, quickly came by the table, bearing water and silverware. Jill got right to it. "Jamie, I'm sorry it took me a minute to recognize you. We're just not used to seeing you in here. It took me a bit to make sure I wasn't at the Waterfront. What's going on?"

"Yeah, I'm working here now," was Jamie's reply. "DW and I decided that it would probably be better if we didn't work together any more. You know, we like being together, but there's a limit."

Jill answered, "Oh, Jamie. Trust me. I understand that. But just wait until you retire. Then you'd better really like each other!"

Hearing that, I raised an eyebrow and gave Jill a questioning look. She, of course, ignored me. I figured that I had either just been insulted or praised. I wasn't sure which. Either way, we are stuck with each other, and that suits me just fine.

Jamie laughed and said, "We'll probably never have to worry about that. I doubt we'll ever be able to retire. Now, what are y'all going to have today?"

She took our order and left for the kitchen.

Shortly, our food was delivered, and our conversation abruptly came to an end. My mullet was fresh, and Jill's hamburger was about as good as they come. As we finished, Jamie came by to deliver the check.

As she laid it on the table, she said, "It's so good to see y'all. I really miss seeing all the regulars at the Waterfront."

"We're going to miss seeing you, too," I replied. "I guess this is just one more in the string of bad things that have been screwing up our happy little island."

"Yeah. I hear you," Jamie answered. "It really does seem like there's been a lot of bad things happening. Speaking of that, have y'all heard about Alan Scharnow?"

"No," I answered. "I don't know that I know him. Is he from the island?"

"Yeah. He used to work for us at the restaurant as a line cook. But a couple of months ago, he disappeared. One day he didn't come in for work, and no one has seen or heard from him since. It's really weird."

"That is strange," I said. "Does he have family on the island?"

"Nope. He's one of those guys, you know, who came down here from the Midwest to avoid the winter and just never managed to go back. He's been down here about five years, lives by himself in a little cracker shack over on Fourth, and uses a bicycle to get around. I don't think he was having money troubles. His rent was paid through the end of the month, but apparently, he just walked off and left it. When we didn't hear from him, we notified the sheriff's office. But they couldn't find out anything about what might have happened to him."

"Wow! Did he have a girlfriend?" I asked. "It's been my experience that when a young guy does something weird like that, there's usually a woman involved. Either that or drugs. Did he seem to have that kind of problem?"

"Not as far as I know on- either score. I never saw him with a girl, and he was always as reliable as you'd want. At the end of the week, once he got paid, he'd head down to Low Key and work his way through a pitcher or two. But as far as I know, that was his only vice."

"Jamie, that's really strange. I'm sorry to hear that. There's just too much weirdness on the island now," I said. "I hate to think about what might happen next."

"Well, hopefully it's all over now," Jamie said. "Let's just think good thoughts, and maybe there won't be a next time. Anyway, thank y'all for coming in. It's really good to see you. See you next time."

Chapter Three

Later that evening, Jill and I attended a party at the island home of some dear friends. Robert and Georgia own a beautiful two-story home, located on a corner lot that backs up onto two of the town's most prestigious canals. As a consequence, Robert is able to have two boat lifts. From one he had hung a Maverick flats skiff; from the other dangled a beautiful center console Contender, perfect for offshore excursions. Robert had it covered. Most of the men in town were more than a little jealous.

The party was outside around their pool. No question, Robert and Georgia had set up their place for hosting great parties. The backyard featured a large, beautiful free-form pool with a Jacuzzi built against one end. In the other direction sat a large tiki hut, which sheltered a fully equipped wet bar. And next to the tiki hut was a small stage, upon which a local band was setting up for the night's gig. Alongside the back of the house, under an overhanging roof, ran a buffet bar equipped with plenty of electrical outlets,

THE CUT BAIT MURDERS

a large sink, a dishwasher, and a commercial-grade icemaker. As I said, parties were not a problem for Robert and Georgia.

The excuse for that night's party was to celebrate the end of "season." Season is the time in Southwest Florida when we are inundated by visitors from the north. It runs from roughly Thanksgiving until Easter. During this period the population of the area quadruples. Some of the visitors own homes in the area; others rent. Some come to stay for the entire period; others only for a few weeks. Regardless, during season, life here changes. It becomes very difficult to get into restaurants, streets are crowded, stores are packed, and boats are everywhere on the sound. To some, season is vital—it's when they make all their money. But to others—those who live here year round and who don't rely on visitors for income—season is a great big pain in the you-know-what. Thus the reason for the party; it was time to celebrate that they had finally all gone home.

Just about all of the town's permanent residents were in attendance. It was great to get to see everyone. During season it was really hard to get together. Some were working all the time. And for those of us who didn't work, it was tough getting together in the bars or restaurants—they were just too crowded. Now, it was like everyone could finally relax and take a deep breath. It was time to enjoy Florida again.

The evening was delightful. The temperature was in the low eighties, with just enough breeze to discourage any insects attracted to the tanned skin of the attendees. However, just to be on the safe side, Georgia had thoughtfully provided enough cans of Deep Woods Off to rout any mosquitoes that might have been able to brave the wind.

Still, despite Georgia's faultless preparations, there remained one nagging issue. Many of the guests were contending with an irritating cough. This symptom was something we had all been dealing with for over a month, courtesy of the worst outbreak of red tide in Southwest Florida's history. Red tide is the common name for when the near-shore waters are inundated by a mass bloom of phytoplankton. These algae are present all the time, but for some unknown reason, they periodically decide to dramatically multiply. When such a bloom happens, a natural toxin is produced in concentrations sufficient to paralyze the central nervous systems of some species of fish and other forms of marine life. This year's outbreak was so bad that not only were fish being killed but our manatee population was also being affected as they breathed the air immediately above the surface of the water—air filled with a high concentration of red tide toxins. Already, in Lee County alone, over two hundred of our "sea cows" had died. This same air, albeit vastly diluted given our distance from the water's surface, was what was causing the cough with which we were contending. Fortunately for humans it was just irritating, not fatal. Just one more thing about life in Saint James City that had taken a darker turn this year.

However, as bad as it was, the air was not bad enough to drive us inside. Neither was it bad enough to keep us from drinking. In fact, I'm pretty sure that drinking was helping to counteract the effect of the toxins in the air. It certainly was helping to make them less noticeable. Robert and Georgia had provided an open bar, and soon the group was deeply into party mode. The ladies had brought hors d'oeuvres, and many in the crowd appeared to be engaged in a migration cycle that kept them moving between the bar and the buffet. Occasionally, however, small groups would break off and stop to catch up on the latest island gossip. Eventually, after several trips to the bar, several folks had gotten up enough nerve to swim in the pool. It promised to be a fun night in Saint James City!

An hour or so later, and several scotch and waters later, I was huddled up with Kenny, Delmar, Eddie, and a couple of other guys near the hot tub. Ostensibly, we were talking about fishing, but the real reason for the gathering was so that we could periodically steal a glance at the very well-endowed, minimally clad twenty-something vixen who was relaxing in the hot tub. Rumor had it that she had come to the party with the band. That kind of made sense; she was definitely putting on a show.

Soon she was joined in the Jacuzzi by a couple of young men who seemed quite intent on getting to know her better. We couldn't help but notice that the guys who got into the hot tub were well on their way to having been over served at the bar. They were certainly feeling no pain. The taller of the two guys was obviously a fan of the art of tattooing. He had had a very large image of a buxom mermaid inked across his back. I thought it had been well done. Kenny told me that these guys were in town for a wedding. They were friends of the son of someone at the party. Someone I didn't know.

Just when the hot tub party was starting to heat up, so to speak, Georgia caught sight of what was going on. She quickly came over to the tub and, in no uncertain terms, ordered everyone out. I suspect she'd had to police that Jacuzzi before. I noticed the girl, after she had gotten out of the pool and dried off, headed inside the house. She came out a few minutes later, having changed into faded frayed jeans and a particularly revealing white blouse. That chick sure knew how to dress for effect. And now, having made sure she was the center of attention, she returned to hanging out with the band.

The guys who had been evicted from the hot tub made another trip to the bar; and a few minutes later, I noticed that they were sitting on a canal-side dock with their legs dangling over the edge. But then I got distracted by a fish tale that someone was spinning, and the next time I noticed, they were gone. I guessed they must have wandered back to one of the bars in town. Or maybe they had simply gone home to sleep it off. I figured either was possible.

Finally, about nine thirty, the crowd started to thin out. We hung around a little while longer, but when the conversation turned to doing shots, we figured it was time we made our exit. Another fun night in Saint James City.

Chapter Four

The next morning we were up early; and after taking care of the dog, we embarked on our customary walk. We have developed a standard three-mile route that took us down along the bay and back through the neighborhood. One of the great things about our walk was that we usually ran into someone we knew. That gave us an opportunity to stop and share island gossip. Usually, that was fun, but the news that day was something we wished we had not learned.

As we headed back up Stringfellow on the return leg of our walk, we ran into Roxie, who was working in her yard. We stopped to chat. Eventually, the conversation turned to what was happening in town, and Roxie said, "Have y'all heard about Terry Wyatt's son?"

Terry Wyatt owned one of the hardware stores on the island. We had met him at the store, but beyond that, we didn't know him.

"No," Jill said. "I didn't really know that Terry even had a son. What happened to him?"

"It's terrible," Roxie said. "His girlfriend found him dead in his bed this morning."

"Damn," we both exclaimed at the same time. "That's awful! What happened?"

"Nobody knows for sure, but everyone is guessing that it was an overdose," Roxie said.

"Shit. I didn't know there was that kind of stuff on Pine Island!" I said.

"Unfortunately, it's here. Especially up around Bokeelia. Lot of bad stuff goes on up there," Roxie said.

"I really hate to hear that. I was hoping that kind of stuff didn't happen on Pine Island," I said. "It's too bad for Terry. That's got to be hard on him."

"Yeah. You know it is."

With that, we said our good-byes and resumed our walk. Our great morning mood had instantly evaporated. Just one more example of the real world intruding into our Pine Island paradise. Drugs on the island, other than pot, were not something we had expected to find here. Time was definitely catching up with the little place it had overlooked.

The rest of the day, everywhere we went, this news was the topic of conversation. And the island's atmosphere, despite the day's bright sun, seemed to have become decidedly gloomy.

Chapter Five

"Have y'all heard about the new clinic up in Little Bokeelia?"

We were having lunch at Woody's, chatting with Adam, who tends bar and manages the place.

"No. What's going on up there?" I replied. "We could certainly use more medical services on the island."

"That's for sure. But this place isn't open to the public. Apparently, it's some kind of place that's just available to high rollers. But it's all pretty hush-hush. I don't know anyone on the island that actually works there."

"Wow. That's different for the island. I didn't know there was anything on Little Bokeelia. Can you get there by road?" I asked.

"No, you can't. There's no bridge. And, it's been privately owned for decades. Way back before World War Two, the island was owned by an inventor, a guy named Charles Burgess. They called it Burgess Island back then. He invented all kind of stuff, but he made his fortune by inventing the dry cell battery. From what I've been told, he and Thomas Edison were good friends.

Supposedly, Edison even planted a lot of the trees that still grow on the island. I went on a field trip to the island when I was a kid. It's really beautiful out there. The house that he built is a gorgeous Spanish manor with over sixty-five hundred square feet of space. I remember being amazed as a kid, having grown up in a single-wide trailer, that any house could be that large—or that pretty. There are also several cottages, a laboratory, pools, koi ponds, and even a waterfall. A wealthy family bought the island back in the nineteen eighties and has kept it up all this time. An uncle of Eddie, the electrician, was the caretaker for the island for the past thirty years. The family put it on the market last year. I think they were asking almost thirty million dollars for the place. To everyone's surprise, it sold pretty quickly. Rumor has it a Spanish doctor bought it and started remodeling a lot of the buildings on the island. But what was strange was that they didn't use any locals to do the construction. In fact, none of the locals could even get on the island. They even fired Eddie's uncle. All the construction materials and all the medical equipment—all European stuff—was staged in Bokeelia and loaded onto barges. The barges were run by Spaniards, and all the construction was done by Spaniards, too. The locals say the workers never left the island the whole time they were building the place. And once it was done, they were put on a private bus, taken to the airport in Punta Gorda, and flown out on a private jet. The whole thing has been kept very quiet. There has never been anything in the *News Press* about it. Nothing on TV, either. I suspect the media doesn't even know it exists."

"Now that is interesting," I exclaimed. "I've got to go take a look at that place. I guess you ought to be able to get up there by boat."

"There are some channels into the island. But I've been told by some of the guides that they've got signs up warning you to stay away, and they've even got some serious-looking guards to make sure you obey their rules."

"Man! That is something," I said. "Who knew? I guess the guy who bought the place must really value his privacy. But if you've got that kind of money, I guess you're entitled to it. Still, I want to see this place. I'm going to take the boat up there and see how far I can get. It sounds like an adventure."

Adam gave me a questioning look and said, "You need to be careful. This whole thing sounds kind of spooky to me. If I were you, I'd make sure that someone knows when you go up there, just to be on the safe side."

"I hear you. I'll be careful, and I'll let you know what I see. Thanks."

Chapter Six

The next morning, over coffee and tea, I said to Jill, "That story about Little Bokeelia Island was something. I'm going to take the boat up there today to get a look at the place. You want to go with me?"

"I'd love to, but I've got a hair appointment this morning. I can't miss that."

"I hear you. What are you getting done to your hair? It looks beautiful to me."

Jill gave me that look, the one meant to convey sympathy that I'm a male. Then she said, "I'm just getting some highlights. Just a little maintenance. You go ahead and get out on the sound. It will do you good. I'll see you at the house this afternoon."

Twenty minutes later I was heading down the canal, on my way to the sound. Saint James City is on the south tip of Pine Island. Little Bokeelia Island is on the northern tip, a distance by water of twenty miles or so. Not a short trip. However, the weather that day was fantastic. Bright sun, a few cumulus clouds, and only a breath of breeze. The temperature was seventy-five and heading toward the low eighties. Perfect conditions for a run up the sound.

The great thing about that time of the year was that all the season folks had gone home, and the summer vacationers hadn't shown up yet. Consequently, it felt like we almost had the sound to ourselves. At least, in a relative sense. Of course that wasn't true, though. That time of the year was the early phase of tarpon fishing season. The good thing about fishing for tarpon at that time was that they were hungry, needing to provision for their upcoming breeding cycle. Therefore, you'd usually find a few anglers on the lower sound, their boats usually anchored in one of the deeper channels, impatiently waiting to hook a silver king. That day was no exception.

The guides loved that time of the year. The good ones were booked solid for a couple of months. And for a guide, that was good money. If a guide's tarpon season was good, then the guide's whole year was good. If you want to catch lots of fish, having a guide is important. However, truthfully, if all you want to do is to jump a tarpon, you don't really need a guide. Anchor in a deep channel in the sound, throw out a large piece of cut mullet or mackerel on a heavy circle hook, and then just let it sit on the bottom. If you've got a strong tidal flow, then the chances are good that you'll hook one. You probably won't land it—only about 20 percent of what you hook will stay connected—but regardless, I guarantee that fighting a tarpon is about the most fun you can have fishing.

That day, as I headed north, I counted seven boats fishing for tarpon. As I went past marker 20, I waved at two guys who had tarpon rods out. I recognized them as canal neighbors. Those two were amazing tarpon fishermen. Every year, they managed to land over a hundred fish. They belonged to the Cape Coral Tarpon Fishing Club, and I'd heard that they always won the Club's trophy. They waved back.

The run up the sound was spectacular. I wished Jill could have been with me. She would have loved it. Not only was it beautiful on the water, but everywhere I looked, wildlife was abundant. Pelicans diving, dolphins rolling, ospreys fishing—just a little of what was about. I even saw a couple of turtles paddling along, and I was especially happy to see a juvenile tarpon jumping for joy. A wonderful morning indeed.

As I went past marker 50, I angled away from the channel, running off to the northeast to follow the deep water east of Useppa Island. From there I followed a marked channel between Patricio and Broken Islands. Then, once I had cleared them, it was an easy run straight to Little Bokeelia.

Charles Burgess had chosen well in selecting his retreat. The island, which sits off the northwest tip of Pine Island, commands a spectacular view of where the northern sound intersects Charlotte Harbor. From the island you can see all the islands that Barron Collier used to own: Useppa, Patricio, and Punta Blanco. You also have a spectacular view of Boca Grande Pass. The westward-facing manor, situated midway on the Y-shaped key, was without doubt sited so that residents would be able to enjoy afternoon sunsets, followed, once the sky darkened, by the reassuring flashes of the Boca Grande lighthouse.

As I came abreast the island, I throttled back the boat, let it settle, and took in the view of the island. "Christ, look at that!" was what I said to myself. The whole island was amazing. It didn't look like anything I had ever seen on Pine Island. Rather, the whole place looked like something that Hollywood might have created as the isolated retreat of a wealthy James Bond villain. The manor was unbelievable. As I looked, I couldn't find anything about it that could have been improved on. A timeless perfection. The island was covered in mature trees, including stately royal palms that surrounded the house. The middle part of the key was dominated by immense banyans. These must have been the trees that Edison had planted on his visits. Under the trees were the various outbuildings, all brilliant in sparkling white paint. Along the shore were several white sand beaches, and there were boat docks on both the west and east sides of the island. But then, as I looked more closely, I got a sense that my initial impression of perfection was not quite right. Something seemed off, something that disturbed the beauty and tranquility of the scene. Finally, I realized what it was. A couple of hundred yards away from shore, mounted on pilings, were a series of large signs that surrounded the island. I could tell that the signs had words on them—something was spelled out in stark red letters painted on a white background—but from where I was, I couldn't make out what they said, so I slipped the Yamaha into gear and eased a little nearer.

Eventually, I could read the sign's red message: *Private Island— Do Not Approach—Violators Will Be Apprehended.* Underneath, it appeared that the same message was repeated in German and Spanish. Clearly, the new owner was serious about his privacy. And if the sign's messages weren't enough to get the point across, I noticed that I was being watched by a guy sitting in a golf cart that was parked on the shore between me and the house. From what I could tell, he looked serious, dressed in black and watching through binoculars. And then, as if that wasn't enough, I could see an array of what looked like long guns standing upright in racks on the sides of the cart.

Still, given that I was there, I figured that I should try to get a better look, so I knocked the engine into gear and eased along to the north. When I reached the marked Jug Creek Channel, I turned and followed it to the east. I knew from looking at the chart that a little further along, another channel branched off to the right, a channel that led into the manor's sheltered boat basin. When I got there, I noticed the same types of signs that I had seen posted in front of the island. However, as far as I knew, the state's navigable waters have always been public. I was pretty sure that a private landowner couldn't legally prevent me from using them. I decided to find out.

It didn't take long. No sooner had I gone past those signs than the guard in the golf cart appeared again. This time he wasn't looking through binoculars. Instead, he was looking at me through the sights of a very deadly-looking weapon. Damn!

"Halt!" The guard said loudly in a voice tinged with what sounded like a German accent. "You may not come through here. This is private. Turn around—now!"

"What are you talking about? You can't prevent me from coming in here to fish. All the waters in the state are public. I saw a school of redfish over by that point, and I'm going to go over there to take a look."

"*Halt*," he said, as if maybe he hadn't said it loudly enough the first time. "Your boat—*now*—will turn around. If you proceed, your boat we will seize, and you detained will be."

I could see that now two additional guards had appeared further up the bay. One was stepping onboard what looked like a military-style inflatable boat. The other, sitting in another golf cart, was apparently just waiting to see what might happen. As I checked them out, I couldn't help but notice a ring mount on the bow of the inflatable. Attached to that was some type of automatic weapon.

"Shit, dude," I said. "I'm just trying to go fishing. Y'all need to chill out. But I don't want any trouble with you, so I'm turning around." I had seen enough. There was nothing to be gained from pushing this confrontation further. Obviously, these folks were serious about keeping uninvited guests off the island.

When I got back to Jug Creek Channel, instead of heading back to the sound, I turned to the right and followed the markers into Bokeelia. A few minutes later, I tied up at the Lazy Flamingo's dock and went inside to get some lunch—and, hopefully, some information.

I took a seat at the bar, ordered a bowl of conch chowder, a dozen oysters on the half shell, and a glass of unsweetened iced tea. As the bartender was shucking the oysters, I engaged him in conversation.

"As I came in, I couldn't help but notice all the signs on Little Bokeelia. What the heck is all that about?" I asked.

"Hey, we're as much in the dark as you are. All I know is that those are some scary-looking dudes guarding the place. Some of the guides have tried to fish around the island, but it didn't take long for them to get the message to get the hell away. Everybody is scared of those guys."

"Yeah, I hear you. I saw some of them as I was coming in. Do any of them ever come in here?" I asked.

"Nope. Never seen any of them in here. As far as that goes, we haven't seen anyone in here from the island since it was sold to that Spanish doctor."

"Jeez," I said. "I heard the island was some kind of clinic. You got any idea what goes on out there?"

"Nope. All I know is that occasionally there are folks coming to, and going from, the island. Sometimes they come in limos to Jug Creek Marina, where they're met by the island's boat, but sometimes they come, or go, by helicopter. One thing for sure: nobody here is getting any business from that place. As far as we're concerned, they're just a pain in the ass."

"I hear you," I said. By that time he was finished with the oysters. He delivered them and the chowder and moved on to other customers. The food was great, as always. I paid the bill, got back in the boat, and headed home. As I went by Little Bokeelia, I noticed that the place looked almost deserted. The only sign of life was a single guard sitting in a golf cart under the shade of a banyan tree.

I didn't wave. Neither did he.

Chapter Seven

"I'll bring the bait; you bring the beer. I'll pick you up at five." With those few words, Kenny and I concluded our planning for the afternoon's tarpon fishing trip. Kenny was a buddy of mine who lived down the canal. He was about my age and recently retired from a career that, among other things, involved building cellular telephone systems. I would guess that his short, wiry frame was an asset when it came to climbing those towers. He may have been slight in stature, but you'd never know it from his voice—it tended to be loud. However, when he was up in the air that was probably an asset, too. And Kenny was almost always fun to be around. I think everybody in town liked him.

The old-timers always said, "If you see white butterflies, it's time to fish for tarpon," and I had noticed butterflies all day. The tide chart showed that there was going to be a strong incoming tide in the afternoon. I figured it was as good a time as any to put the white butterfly myth to the test.

By five thirty we were anchored in twenty-one feet of water in the channel by Sanibel. We were fishing with cut bait, large pieces of Spanish mackerel, embedded on forged fourteen-aught circle hooks. Medium-heavy rods, five thousand series reels, fifty-pound braided line, with hundred-pound mono leaders...strong tackle for strong fish. There was a full moon that night, so the tide was stronger than usual. Conditions couldn't be more perfect for catching tarpon.

It didn't take long to get some action. We were fishing our baits right on the bottom, weighted down with two-ounce oval sinkers which were able to slide on short pieces of leader tied between heavy-duty swivels. Maybe twenty minutes after we put our baits out, my line took off at a right angle to the current. The rod bowed deeply, and line started to zing off the reel, despite the heavy drag that had been set. I grabbed the rod and leaned back against the strain. With a circle hook, you don't set the hook by jerking the rod like you do with a traditional hook. Instead, you let the hook set itself when the fish pulls against you. That day, when the fish felt the tip of the hook, he exploded straight out of the water, shaking his head from side to side, attempting to throw the painful metal from his mouth. Unfortunately, that was exactly what he did. My fight with this silver king lasted all of fifteen seconds. Regardless, I was shaking with excitement as I laid the rod down.

"Damn, Kenny! Did you see that? I bet he jumped ten feet in the air. That was something."

"Hot diggity, hot diggity dog! They are in here, all right," Kenny said. "Come on, fishy, fishy, fishy, get on *my* line."

It didn't take long for Kenny to have his incantation answered. About ten minutes later, his line took off just like mine had. This time, Kenny's fish jumped five times before throwing the hook.

All the while we were fishing, we could see tarpon of all sizes rolling around us. It was truly a great day for fishing. I think the white butterfly myth was confirmed.

We kept fishing. I jumped two more fish and landed a big shark. Kenny jumped three fish as well. However, neither of us had been able to bring a tarpon alongside the boat. But a little after six thirty, that changed. I was finally able to land a huge tarpon. It must have weighed 160 pounds. It took me a little over fifty-three minutes to bring it to the side of the boat and release it. Fighting a fish that large, for that long, really does a number on you. My back hurt. My forearms were in knots. I was whipped. Maybe a younger man would have been able to continue fishing, but this retired sixty-four-year-old was ready to head home.

"Kenny," I said, "that bastard wore me out. I'm done. You ready to go in?"

"What's the matter with you, big guy? One little fish like that is all you can handle? I figured a stud like you would be good for three or four tarpon in a day."

"Maybe once upon a time," I replied. "But don't forget that big bull shark I pulled in just before I hooked the tarpon. That was a thirty-minute struggle. I'd think you'd give me some credit for that one, too."

"Yeah, I guess that counts. And besides, you *are* an old fart. I can understand why you need to go lie down and rest for a while."

"Who are you calling an old fart, you miserable old coot? If I remember correctly, you're a year older than me."

About then I noticed that Kenny's line was tightening and slowly moving in the same direction as the tide. Kenny grabbed his rod and began to reel. "Damn, Jim. I've got something. Something big!"

He leaned against the rod a couple of times to make sure the hook was set, then continued to reel. However, it quickly became clear that whatever was on the other end of the line was not running, and it was not stripping off line against the drag. If it had been a tarpon, once it had felt the hook, it would have taken off like a Saturn Five, smoking line off the reel and jumping toward the sky. This thing, though, was just sitting there. But it was big; that was clear from the way Kenny was struggling to winch it toward the boat. Still, it didn't seem to be moving. It was just sitting there.

"Kenny, what the hell have you got?" I asked.

"Damn, Jim. I don't know. It ain't a tarpon, that's for sure. And it's not a shark. It's just hugging the bottom and moving with the tide. Maybe it's a manta ray. There are some big ones out here."

"Yeah. I've seen some of 'em jumping. I'd bet they're ten feet across. I think I hooked one once. But it just kind of sucked to the bottom, and then, every once in a while, it would swim a little. I never could get it off the bottom. Finally, I got impatient trying to get it up, put too much pressure on it, and broke the line. Has that thing you've got moved any?"

"I don't think so, Jim. I haven't felt it fight at all. But it's heavy, I can tell you that—probably more than a hundred pounds. But it feels kind of like a dead weight. Still, I'm making progress. I lift the rod, and then I wind down on the reel. I get six feet every time. I'll have it up in a couple of minutes. I want to see what it is."

I know that Kenny thought then that he wanted to see what was on his hook, but I'm pretty sure he changed his mind when it finally broke the surface.

"Shit, Jim. What the fuck is that?"

"Oh my God," was all I could reply. "Oh my God!"

What was on the hook was not a fish. What was on the hook was a human body. Or at least what was left of what had once been a human body, before the sharks and the crabs had gotten to it. And before someone had slit the torso from chest to groin.

"Kenny, do you recognize that tattoo?" I asked.

"Shit, it looks like the guy who was in the hot tub at Robert and Georgia's," said Kenny.

"Yeah," I answered. "I guess he must have really pissed off one of the guys in the band."

"He sure pissed off somebody," Kenny answered. "Now, what do we do with him?"

Chapter Eight

"Lee County Sheriff, Lee County Sheriff, this is the *Pulapanga*, over."

"Boat calling Lee County Sheriff, acknowledge and go to channel six eight."

"Lee County Sheriff, this is *Pulapanga*. Going to six eight."

Once I had switched to the working channel, I answered "Lee County, *Pulapanga*, over."

"*Pulapanga*, go ahead."

"Lee County, we're fishing in Sanibel Channel, and just pulled in a man's body. Y'all need to get here in a hurry. Over."

"*Pulapanga*, what do you mean, you pulled in a man's body? Is the man injured? Over."

"Yeah. He's injured all right. He's dead! Y'all need to get here, now. Bring Mike Collins with you. We'll be waiting on you. Over and out." Mike Collins was the chief detective in the Gulf Islands division of the Lee County sheriff's department. He had been the lead investigator in the Carl Perez affair, and I knew he was a good guy.

"Kenny, I think we need to put a rope around him, just in case your line breaks, or the hook pulls out. Let me get a dock line ready and then pull him over closer to the side of the boat."

"Take your time, Jim. He ain't going anywhere."

As Kenny pulled him closer, I slipped the bight of a dock line through the swaged end, making a good size slip loop, which I dropped over what was left of the body's arms and upper torso. I pulled the loop tight, and tied the line off on one of the boat's aft mooring cleats. Next, we cut the leader to the hook. There was no way either of us wanted to touch the dead guy to get the hook out. Then, we waited.

Twenty minutes later we saw a flashing blue light coming out the Caloosahatchee channel, known locally as the "Miserable Mile." The boat it was attached to appeared to be headed our way. Soon, we could make it out as a Lee County inflatable, with four deputies onboard. As it approached, I waved it in our direction.

"Damn, Story! Just when I thought I had seen the last of you. What is it with you and bodies? You some kind of Jonah or something?"

"Lieutenant Collins," I answered. "It's really good to see you, too."

"Fuck that, what do you have?"

I introduced Kenny, and together we walked through what had transpired. "We've got the body, or what's left of it, tied off on the starboard side. But there's something you ought to know. We think we know who this is."

"That's a start. Who is it?"

34

"Well, we don't actually know his name, but we saw him at a party in Saint James City a couple of days ago. We recognize his tattoo. Supposedly, he was in town for the wedding of one of his buddies. At the party, he was messing around with this really hot chick. But I think she was taken, so to speak, by one of the guys who was playing in the band. Maybe after the party, things got out of hand, and the guy in the band went after this dude with a knife."

By this time, the sheriff's boat had moved to where the deputies had a good view of the body.

Lieutenant Collins replied, "I don't think so. This doesn't look like a crime of passion. It looks to me like this guy was professionally butchered."

An hour later the deputies were through with us. The sheriff's crime scene unit was processing what evidence there was, and the body was on its way to the morgue. Kenny and I headed home.

Chapter Nine

The next night Jill and I were sitting at the bar in the American Legion, enjoying our five-dollar pizza and a couple of cheap drinks. The Legion was one of the places in town where a lot of folks ended up spending some time. Not only could you eat and drink there very inexpensively, but there was also usually something fun going on. Tuesday night was bingo; Thursday night was karaoke. However, nothing was scheduled this particular night. Consequently, it was quiet, with only about a dozen folks sitting around the bar.

As we ate, we chatted with the lady who was tending the bar. The topic of conversation, of course, was the recently discovered body. The sheriff's guys had been in town all day, trying to find out as much as they could about who the guy was, why he was in town, and what he had been doing.

"So, Shannon," I asked the bartender, "did you know the guy?"

"No. I don't think so. The deputies came in here with a picture of the guy that they'd gotten somewhere, but I had never seen him in here. They also asked me if I knew anything about the guys in the band."

"Do you know them?"

"Yeah. They play here about once a month."

"Do they ever have a hot chick with them? A real cute little piece that seems to enjoy being a tease?"

Shannon laughed. "You must mean Tina. She's always here with the band. She's married to the lead singer. Rumor has it that he really gets turned on by seeing other guys hitting on her. But there's never been any trouble in here. No offense, but you know how it is—there's never anyone in here young enough to take her too seriously. Some of the old farts sometimes get a little excited, but their wives straighten them out in a hurry. It's really kind of cute."

"Damn. That kind of hurts," I said.

"Don't you worry, honey," Shannon said. "I've heard some of the blue hairs in here talking about you. They really like your ponytail."

Jill laughed.

To change the subject, I asked Shannon, "What's going on with Tommy down at the other end of the bar? It looks like he's not doing too good."

"I don't think he is. He's been this way for about a week. He doesn't say anything to anyone. Just comes in every night, starts to drink, and keeps it up until we kick him out. We're thinking about pulling his bar privilege. We don't want him leaving here one night and hurting someone on the road."

"I hear you," I said. "Y'all have to be careful about that kind of thing. But I hate to see Tommy like that. He's a good guy. He must have something bothering him—probably one of his girlfriends dumped him. But I'm sure he'll find another one soon. It seems like he's got a different girl every other time I see him."

"That's Tommy," Shannon said. "Y'all ready for your check?"

"Yeah. We need to get home before nine o'clock so we don't miss our bedtimes."

Chapter Ten

As I was signing the charge slip, I noticed Tommy get off his stool. I figured he was heading for the restroom, but I was wrong.

"Jim Story! I heard you found a body yesterday."

I could tell that he'd been drinking. He was speaking a little louder than necessary, and there was the slightest hint of a slur to his words.

"Yeah, Tommy. I did."

"Well, at least, fuck, it wasn't my brother. When I heard about it I was scared shitless that it was him. But thank God, it wasn't. I just wish the hell I knew where he was."

"Tommy, what's going on with your brother?" I said.

"Fuck. I wish I knew. All I know is that he's fucking disappeared. Damn, it's like he's just vanished. I saw him one day about a week ago, and everything was absolutely normal. But I haven't fucking seen him since. No one has. I'm worried that something has happened to him."

It was at this point that Tommy apparently finally noticed that Jill was sitting with me. "Sorry, ma'am, for my language," he apologized. "I'm just worried about my brother, and I guess I've been drinking a little bit."

"Tommy, don't you worry about it. It's not the first time I've heard four-letter words. And I'm sorry to hear about your brother," Jill said. "Does he live with anyone?"

"No. He isn't married, just lives by himself in a trailer up on the way to Bokeelia. He works odd jobs whenever someone needs an extra hand. Yard work, construction, that kind of thing. Everyone running a business on the island knows where to find him, and they pick him up whenever they need help on a job. Otherwise, he just rides around on his bicycle. We always get together about once a week and drink some beers. Otherwise, he's always kept to himself."

"Damn. That doesn't sound good," I said. "But hopefully, he'll show up. Maybe he just went off island for a while."

"I was hoping so, but now I don't think so. I found his dog a couple of days ago. She was up at Jug Creek Marina, just sitting by the dock. I took her home with me, but now the dog's gone again. I don't know what's going on, Jim, but I don't think it's good. I was hoping I'd run into you. I know you found out about what Carl Perez was up to, so I was hoping you might be able to help me find out what's happened to my brother."

"Tommy, have you gone to the sheriff's office with this? That's what you need to do."

"Yeah. I filed a fucking missing person's report with them, and they put it out on the statewide missing person's web site. But it seems like that's about all they're going to do. They just didn't seem all that concerned that a Pine Island day laborer had disappeared. I think they thought it was par for the course. That's why I was hoping that you might be able to help," Tommy said.

"Tommy, I'm not a detective. I don't know that I can really be of any help. But if I hear anything, I'll let you know. But Tommy, I've got to tell you, I don't like the sound of this. I think you're right to be worried about your brother."

Chapter Eleven

As we drove home, Jill said, "All right, that's just too damn strange. There's definitely something going on out here. First, Jamie tells us about their cook who disappeared. Then there's the kid you and Kenny fished up. Now its Tommy's brother. And don't forget Terry Wyatt's son. I wonder if this all has something to do with drugs."

"It might. Whatever it is, I don't like it. The island's just not the way it used to be."

Jill replied, "I agree. Maybe you ought to talk with Mike Collins."

"I think I will. I'll give him a call in the morning."

In the morning I called Lieutenant Collins's cell phone. I still had his number from dealing with him six months previously. He answered on the second ring.

"Damn, Story. This is like a bad dream. I thought I was through with you, but you just keep coming back. And no, I haven't yet figured out who carved up the kid in the bay. I assume that's why you're calling."

"Mike, I'm so glad you've still got your cheerful disposition. That's one of the things I always have liked about you. It's so refreshing to deal with a public servant that has a great attitude. But no, I wasn't calling to ask if you'd solved the case yet." (I thought about adding that I had dealt with him enough to know that that would have been an unrealistic expectation, but I figured that might have been pushing our relationship a little too far.) "Actually, Mike, I was just hoping that we could get together for a few minutes. I want to tell you about some stuff that's going on out here. Who knows? It might be of some help to you."

"Coming from anyone other than you, Story, I might be insulted. But, since you solved my last case for me and made me look like a hero in the process, I'm willing to cut you some slack. How about lunch at the Waterfront?"

"Sounds good. I'll see you at noon."

I pedaled my bike the five blocks to the Waterfront. It was a great little restaurant on the southern tip of Pine Island, housed in a building constructed in 1910 as the original schoolhouse for Saint James City. It still had a little of that vibe. As I coasted into the parking lot, I noticed a dark, blacked-out SUV with inconspicuous electronics on the roof. I figured this for Mike Collin's new ride. I pushed open the heavy front door of the restaurant, admiring as I did its bronze porthole window, and walked in.

Dee, one of the long-term wait staff, gave me a smile and pointed to the deck. "He's waiting for you out back."

So much for there being any secrets on the island. I guess it really is a small town.

"Hey, Mike. How's it going?" I asked, as I slid onto the bench seat at the table in the shade where he was sitting near the south end of the deck.

"Oh, you know. Just another day, another murder. How's Jill?"

"She's good. At least as good as she can be, having to put up with me."

"I hear that. I've always wondered how *you* manage to keep a beautiful lady like her happy. You make sure to let her know that if she ever gets ready to upgrade, I'm available."

I laughed. "I'll be sure to let her know. But you better be careful making offers like that. She might just take you up on it."

"Nah. She's got too much sense for that. Now what's up?"

"Mike, I just wanted to make sure you know that there is some weird stuff going on here on the island. I don't know if it has anything to do with the guy in the bay or not, but something's going on out here that's not quite right." I knew as soon as I had said it that I had opened the door for Mike to again lecture me with his tongue-in-cheek opinion concerning those of us who lived on Pine Island. At least, I thought it was tongue-in-cheek. I wasn't to be disappointed.

"Shit, Story. If you got me out here just to let me know that folks on Pine Island aren't quite right, you could have saved us both the trip. I'm surprised that you're just figuring that out. I thought everybody already knew that. Folks out here haven't ever been normal. I think that's probably the real reason the Calusa left. From what I've been told, Ponce de Leon marooned some of his troublesome crew on Pine Island. Unfortunately, they not only survived, but they multiplied. I know for a fact that's why the county has ever only built one bridge out here. That way we can keep an eye of all you inmates that live in this asylum. Why don't you tell me something I don't already know?"

"Cute, Collins. I feel so much better knowing that you've got my back. But hear me out. If you'll shut your mouth and open your ears, you might actually learn something—as unusual as that might be."

With our convivialities out of the way, I commenced to tell him about the folks on the island who had disappeared and about the other tragedies that had recently taken place.

"Jim, welcome to my world. That's what I live with every day. You know, it sounds to me kind of like reality. I know you like to think that Saint James City is a magic place that's immune to the shit that infects the rest of Lee County, but trust me, it's not. Folks disappear everywhere, every day. Have you taken a look at how long the missing persons list is, just for our area? Last time I looked at it there were over a hundred names on it. People disappear for all kinds of reasons. Sometimes they're in debt; sometimes they've got trouble with a woman; maybe they're behind on their alimony; sometimes it's drugs; sometimes they just decide to fucking move on. Truthfully, about the only time we take them seriously is when it involves a young kid, some old fart with Alzheimer's who has wandered off into the bushes, or when there's a clear indication of foul play. A couple of deadbeats who live in dilapidated trailers and ride bicycles usually don't get a lot of our attention. Is that wrong? Maybe. Hell, probably. But Jim, I hate to burst your bubble, that's reality. We don't have the resources to go looking every time somebody decides to take a hike."

With that, Lieutenant Collins leaned back and looked into my eyes. I thought I could detect a challenging look.

"Take it easy, Mike" I said. "I'm not criticizing. I just want you to know that there's something weird going on out here. What about the drug overdose? You think that might be related to any of this?"

"Who knows? That's always a possibility. But I'd guess the OD was just an accident. The thing we're seeing a lot of now involves prescription pills. Oxycontin and stuff like that is a huge problem. People don't think of them as being dangerous, but pills are by far the most lethal drug problem we have to deal with. I'd bet that for every person who ODs on smack or coke, we see ten that take too many feel-goods. You mix in a little booze, and it can easily be lights out. And it's a problem everywhere, even here on the island. In fact, we've got our eye on a place between here and Center that seems to be writing a lot of prescriptions for pain. Hell, it's hard to prove, though. I don't know if you know, but a couple of years back we put away a guy who lived right down the canal from you. He was a legitimate doctor from Miami, but on the side, he was writing pill mill prescriptions. He used the cash to buy that huge house down by the bay. I can tell you, he used to throw some really big parties out there. But now he's up in Starke. Not going to be doing any partying for another eleven years. But that kind of shit's going on everywhere. Yeah, drugs are always a possibility. Did your guys that disappeared have that kind of problem?"

"Not that I've heard. From what I was told, they were both reliable and pretty sober. But I don't know if they would have told me that, even if it was true."

"Look, Jim. I appreciate you telling me this. I'll keep it in mind as we're poking around. If I find anything interesting, I'll let you know. But don't hold your breath. You ready to order lunch?"

We both ordered Caesar salads with grilled fish. Mike asked for grouper; I went for triggerfish. Once that was out of the way, we resumed our conversation.

All right, Mike. I know you haven't figured out who did the guy we pulled up, but what are you thinking that might be about?" I asked.

"Jim, I don't know. It's a strange deal. It wasn't a crime of passion. When our Doc did the autopsy he said it looked like the poor guy had been cut up by a surgeon. It wasn't like he'd been slashed up. Just very neat incisions."

"That's weird," I said. "Any thoughts on why he was in the channel?"

"My guess is that whoever put him there was counting on the sharks and crabs to dispose of the body. I'd bet that he was dropped in further out in the bay, out where nobody ever fishes much, but this week's extra strong tides caused him to drift up the channel to where you guys were fishing. I think it was just an accident that y'all hooked him before the sharks and crabs could finish their jobs."

"I don't know, Mike. Wouldn't the body have floated? That sounds to me like a poor way to dispose of a body."

"I asked the doc the same thing. It's been my experience that a dead body starts to float after about a week. But he said he didn't think that would have been the case with our guy. Usually, a body floats when decomposition gets going and gases build up in the abdominal cavity. But in this case, all the organs, stomach, and intestines had been removed, and the abdominal cavity had been opened up. It was his opinion that the body would have likely stayed on the bottom if you guys hadn't hooked him."

"OK, I'll buy that," I said. "Let me tell you something about the girl who was in the hot tub with the guy we found. According to the bartender down at the Legion, she likes to tease whenever the band she hangs out with is playing. Apparently, the lead singer has some kind of kinky thing about that. Seeing her hitting on other guys turns him on, or something. Hell, maybe it makes him sing more passionately."

"Yeah," Mike laughed. "We know all about Tina. She has caused more than her share of trouble. It's not so bad out here on the island, but when the band plays out in Lehigh, watch out! She's caused a couple of knife fights out there. We've warned her and her friend to cool the act. And I think they have, to some extent. But I guess they can only go so long before they need to get another hit of excitement. Regardless, I don't think that they did our hot tub guy. We're looking into what the Vic did while he was down here and all that stuff, but so far we've got nothing. As far as anyone knows, he was just having a good time. Probably just going fishing during the day and getting drunk at night. Pretty typical behavior for a guy his age. We've learned that the night he disappeared, he got drunk at Froggy's, just hanging out by himself. The folks there say he left the bar about midnight, and that was the last time anyone saw him."

"Wasn't he here for a wedding? Why didn't they report him missing?"

"The wedding took place a couple of days before he disappeared. Everyone else had already gone home. But apparently he had decided to stay a little longer, for some reason."

"I wonder why that was," I said.

"I'm wondering the same thing. Why, in your opinion, would a guy his age decide to stay in Saint James City?" asked Mike.

"Probably because he wanted to go fishing."

"That'd be my guess," Mike answered. "But who knows—maybe he met a girl."

"In Saint James City?" I asked.

"Hey, there're some good-looking ladies here."

"Yeah," I answered, "but most of them are over sixty. My good-looking wife, of course, excepted."

"Guess I'd better start to investigate Jill, then."

"I'll let her know to expect your visit. She'll be flattered."

Mike laughed. "I doubt that. But look, Jim, I appreciate the information. I'll let you know if we get anything on the disappearances. See you later."

Chapter Twelve

"Are we doing appetizers tonight at Froggy's?" Jill texted Carolyn.

"Yes. See you there," Carolyn replied.

One of the issues for the bars in Saint James City during "off season" was that there isn't enough business during the week to justify staying open. The owners had minimum expenses to cover—salaries, costs to air condition and light the place, and so on. So most of them just stay closed. The problem with this, though, was that if the bars were closed, there weren't any places where the locals could meet to socialize. In most parts of the country, this wouldn't really be a problem, but in a tiny, quiet, end-of-the-road fishing village with a significant population of semi-alcoholic retirees whose chief source of entertainment was hanging out at a bar and chatting with their friends, it was a major issue. To address this, the locals who frequented Froggy's had come up with a unique solution. On the slowest night of the week, they each brought an appetizer dish to the bar, arriving a little after five. That way none of them had to worry about either the effort or the cost of cooking dinner at home. And, of course, they bought beer and drinks while they were at the bar. It was a win-win for all concerned. The bar made enough money to stay open, and the locals had a place to gather, eat, and catch up on what went on over the weekend. So, of course, that's where Jill and I headed this particular night.

We arrived fashionably late, around five thirty, adding Jill's delicious cheese and sausage dip to the food already on the table. By six, the place was packed, and the noise level in the bar had reached the level of a good buzz. Everyone was chatting, drinking, and eating. I was talking with Kenny and Steve Fairchild, the ex-army ranger who, the previous year, had covered me as we lured Carl Perez into the trap that eventually cost Carl his life. Steve was a good guy. Tonight, he wanted to catch up on what was happening with the investigation into the death of the guy Kenny had pulled up in the sound.

"What is it with you, Story?" Steve asked. "I go my whole life and never get anywhere near a murder. Then I start hanging out with you, and people start getting knocked off, one after another. I'm beginning to think it's not a good idea to be seen with you."

"Damn, Steve! It's taken you this long to figure that out? Most women I meet are able to pick up on that right away!"

"I don't doubt that," Steve joked. "But what's going on with this one?"

I filled them in on what I had learned from Mike Collins. They were particularly interested in why the guy was hanging out in town after the wedding. I told them I figured he must have been going fishing. Kenny chimed in, "Jerry just came in. Let's see if he knows anything." He waved him over.

Jerry was one of the town's better fishing guides. And he was good buddies with Hector, the best—and busiest—guide. When he was booked, Hector would direct any client overflows in Jerry's direction. I figured that if someone had been staying in town to go fishing with a guide, Jerry would know. When he came over, we quickly brought him up to speed.

"Nah. He didn't go fishing with me. In fact, I was pretty slow all week. But I know for a fact that Hector had the same two doctors on his boat for three days. I doubt that this dead kid wanted to hire a guide. Otherwise, I would have heard about it."

"Maybe he rented a boat and went fishing on his own," Kenny said.

Steve spoke up. "Let's ask Katie. She's been working at the marina. She'd probably know." With that he waved at his wife, motioning for her to come over. She headed in our direction, bringing Jill and a couple of the other girls with her.

"Hello, ladies!" Kenny exclaimed. "Yes, I am available later. But I can only handle one of you beauties at a time. So, who wants to be first?"

"Kenny, you're so full of shit!" Katie exclaimed. "It's a good thing that you're so cute. What's up, guys?"

Steve answered, "We're trying to find out if the dead kid might have rented a boat last week at the marina. Katie, you were running the office. Did he rent a boat?"

"No, I'm sure he didn't. We only rented two boats all week. One was to a couple from Lake Wales. They were probably in their sixties. The other was to two Baptist ministers. One is from Labelle, and the other is from Clewiston. They come over once a month to go fishing. They've done that for a decade. Why do you want to know if he rented a boat?"

"Well," Steve responded, "we're just trying to figure out why that guy was still in town. He had come down for a wedding, but he stayed on after everyone else had gone."

"That's easy," Katie answered.

We looked at her, dumbfounded. "What do you mean?" I asked.

"If it's the guy I'm thinking of, he was here so he could hang out with Jennifer," Katie answered. "Was he the blond-haired guy with the mermaid tattoo?"

"Yeah, that was the guy," I answered.

"He had a crush on Jennifer," Katie said.

"You mean Jennifer who dips shrimp at the marina on the weekend?" Steve asked.

"Of course. Jennifer, with the long, long dancer's legs, the short, short shorts, and the lovely young sweet sixteen face. Heck, every Saturday we've got old coots coming in there to buy bait who don't even own a fishing rod. Y'all all know who I'm talking about, and don't pretend you don't."

"Oh, her!" we all answered in unison, trying to sound as innocent as possible.

"Yeah. He met her at the wedding and had been hitting on her all week. She'd not wanted anything to do with him but finally agreed to go out one night last week, just to try to get rid of him. But from what she told me, he never showed to pick her up. She was pretty steamed about that."

"Steamed enough to cut him up and dump him in the bay?" Kenny asked.

"Oh, come on." With a wink, Katie said to Kenny, "The only person I ever heard her threaten with that was you."

We all laughed as Kenny turned red.

"What about her father?" I asked.

"I doubt it could be him. He had surgery on his ankle a couple of weeks ago, and he has to use a knee scooter just to get around. Can't even drive a car. I doubt he'd be able to whack anyone, cut him open, and dump him in the bay. And besides, according to what Jennifer told me, the dead guy never did anything to her other than stand her up. I don't think that would rise to the level of justifying a homicide."

"What about a jealous boyfriend?" I asked.

"No," Katie said. "I know Jennifer pretty well. I'm sure she's never had a serious relationship. She's really a good kid. Just trying to make some money before she leaves for Gainesville in the fall. I'm sure there's nothing to that."

"Probably not," I said. "Look, we're not getting anywhere figuring out who killed this guy. If he just stayed in town because he had a crush on a teenage girl, that really doesn't help us much."

"Hey, Sherlock," Jill said. "Let me remind you that it's not your job to solve this. You and Kenny fished the guy up, but that doesn't mean that y'all are obligated to find out who did it. In fact, Jim, your only obligation is to keep me happy. And to do that right now, you need to go over to the bar and get me another beer."

I gave her a wink and headed in that direction.

Chapter Thirteen

The next morning, Jill and I were sitting on the screened porch. Whenever the weather permitted, we loved to sit in our Adirondacks, drink tea, read the paper, and enjoy the glories of Southwest Florida. And that morning was especially glorious. A Bermuda high had stalled over the state. As a result the air was dryer and cooler than usual, and there wasn't a cloud in the sky. It was the kind of morning that reminded us of why we had moved to Saint James City.

However, as I soon learned, that day Jill wasn't all that happy that we were here.

"What would you think about going down to the Keys for a few days?" Jill asked.

I didn't answer. In fact, I was dumbstruck. I had never before heard her express any interest in going to the Keys. Finally, I asked, "With you?"

"Of course, with me!" Jill responded. "Who else would you be going to the Keys with?"

"OK. You know as long as I'm with you I'll go anywhere."

"That's a good one," Jill replied. "I'll put that one in the little book where I keep track of the very few romantic things you've ever said or done. But look—I'm serious. I want to get you out of town before you get any more involved in trying to solve whatever's going on. You almost managed to get yourself killed the last time you started acting like Barnaby Jones. What do you say we just give it a rest, and let the professionals do their jobs?"

If there's one thing I'd learned from being married to Jill, it was that when she said something like she had just said, I had better pay attention. The only excuse for doing otherwise would be if I had a really good reason to ignore her. And today, I didn't have that kind of reason. True, I was certainly interested in what was going on here on the island, and why. However, unlike when Carl Perez had killed my friend Jorge, this time I didn't have a dog in the fight. It was probably a good idea for me to get out of town.

"OK. Going to the Keys sounds like fun. Where do you want to go?"

"Jim, I've never been to Key West, and I've always wanted to go. What would you think about going there?"

"That would be cool. We could even take the Key West Express that runs out of Fort Myers Beach."

Jill replied, with a note of caution in her voice, "What is the Key West Express?"

"It's a fast ferry. It makes a round trip run to Key West four or five times a week. I've heard it only takes about four hours to get there. Kenny told me that he had taken it a couple of years ago. He said it was fun."

"Sounds like an adventure," Jill responded.

I could tell she was warming up to my idea. So I figured that while I was on a roll, I'd add another. "What about going out to see Fort Jefferson while we are there?"

"Where is that?" Jill asked. She'd known me long enough to know better than to accept any of my ideas without some degree of skepticism.

"It's in the Dry Tortugas, which are about fifty miles west of Key West. The only way to get there is either by boat or by seaplane."

"What's so special about this fort?" she asked.

"First, it is beautiful out there. This fort just sits out there in the middle of the gulf on what looks like nothing more than a sandbar. It's really an amazing place to see. Second, it's full of history. It's where they kept prisoners during and after the Civil War. In fact, it's where they kept Dr. Mudd after he was convicted of tending to John Wilkes Booth. It's a cool place. I'd like you to see it."

"Did you say that you could get there by seaplane?" she asked.

"Yeah. I think it only takes about thirty minutes in the air. What would you think about that?"

"I'd like that a lot. I'll always remember the seaplane ride we took when we went to Vancouver Island. That was cool."

All right. Let's do it. You find us a place to stay, and I'll work on the transportation issues."

Twenty minutes later the plans were in place. We were going down early the next morning. I'd even arranged for a limo service to pick us up at the house so that we wouldn't have to leave the car at the port.

By five thirty in the morning, we had loaded our bags in the trunk of the Lincoln town car waiting in our driveway. We'd used this same service ever since we'd bought the house, and they'd always done a great job. The service was owned by a married couple, Tom and Alice. Tom was a good guy; he just didn't talk much. Alice, on the other hand, enjoyed chatting with her passengers. That morning Tom was driving, which was probably a good thing since we were still a little too sleepy to really enjoy engaging in a conversation. In a little less than an hour, he was unloading our bags next to the ferry's gangway.

"Y'all have a great trip. Just try to stay out of trouble."

I suspected that Tom may have been concerned with the thermos of Bloody Marys that Jill and I had brought with us—and which we had already emptied. "You don't have to worry about us," I answered. "Early to rise, early to bed. That's our motto."

"Well, y'all just make sure you have a good time. Alice will be here to pick you up when you get back. She'll be parked across the street, and as soon as she sees you, she'll pull right here to pick you up."

"Great. Thanks for the ride."

With that, we gave our bags and tickets to the guy manning the booth and headed aboard. Twenty minutes later the crew let go the lines, and the trip was underway.

Four days later, the Key West Express, with us onboard, eased back into its Fort Myers berth. Jill and I had enjoyed a truly wonderful break. We may not have done everything there was to do in Key West, but we'd done our best to do most of them. We had made the trip to the Dry Tortugas. We'd gone fishing one day. We'd ridden the Conch Train. We'd enjoyed the sunset and craziness of Mallory Square. And, of course, we had spent a lot of time on Duval Street. It was time for us to come home, and we were ready. We needed to dry out!

As promised, as we came down the gangway, we saw Alice waiting across the street. She had the car alongside the curb by the time we got there. Jill gave Alice a big hug. Minutes later she and Jill were engaged in girl talk as she steered us toward Pine Island. They talked about our trip and about all that we had done. Then they started talking about their grandbabies. That conversation took a while. In the meantime, I was trying to work up a much-needed nap. But when I heard Alice mention the new clinic in Bokeelia, I came awake.

"I've recently had a number of trips to Bokeelia, taking folks to the new clinic, or picking them up," Alice was saying.

With that, I spoke up. "Alice, we've heard about the clinic, but no one on the island really knows that much about it. Did your passengers tell you about it?"

"Not really. But I'll tell you this: the folks using that clinic are wealthy. They always come into, or out of, Punta Gorda Jet Port, and they're always flying private. And most of them—heck, I guess all of them—are European, so it's not been easy to chat. And besides, none of them act like they want to talk to me," Alice said.

I asked, "Can you tell if they're sick when they go out there?"

"Yeah, they've been pretty feeble."

"Alice, how about when you pick them up?"

"You know, that's kind of funny. Sometimes they look sick. Sometimes, not so much. Who knows? Maybe the clinic is helping some of them."

"Well," I said, "hopefully it is. But to me, it all sounds kind of strange."

"You can say that again," Alice replied.

By that time, we were pulling into Saint James City. A few minutes later, Alice had pulled our bags out of the trunk, and we had said our good-byes. We were home.

Chapter Fourteen

We spent the next couple of days catching things up around the house. Jill worked on the laundry we had brought back with us, and I focused on the outside of the house. Living in the tropics, there's always a list of outdoor chores needing to be done, most of which involve dealing with the explosive plant growth resulting from the combination of sunshine, rain, and heat. For example, there are always palm fronds and coconuts to deal with. And the deck that runs around the house frequently needs attention from a pressure washer to remove the bougainvillea and hibiscus blossoms that tend to accumulate there when they fall. But at least when working in the yard, I can also work on my tan.

The days passed happily. And truthfully, it was not all work, no play. Each afternoon we made a point of retiring to the pool, where we floated while enjoying our well-earned beverages of choice. Yes. Retired life can be great. And for the most part, we managed to put the island's mysteries out of our mind...but that changed on Monday.

Mondays in Saint James City were always special, and not only because Monday signified that we had survived the weekend. Just as important was the fact that it was dollar taco day at the American Legion. And with that, of course, it was understood that it was also dollar margarita day. So for four or five dollars, we could have a really great lunch! We could also mingle with our friends and neighbors who recognized a bargain when they saw one.

Jill and I were sitting at one of the high-top tables in the back corner. I was enjoying my third taco and my second salt-rimmed, tequila-infused, lime-flavored beverage. Jill was lagging behind by one—in both categories. Just as I licked my fingers to rid them of the flavorful combination of meat grease and tomato juice that dribbled onto them as I finished my taco, I felt a hand on my shoulder. Turning, I saw that it belonged to Tommy. I could see that he didn't look too good. In fact, he looked to me like he had probably been drunk since the last time we'd met.

"Tommy," I said. "How are you doing?"

"Fuck, Jim. How does it look like I'm…doing?" Tommy slurred.

I could tell that he had reached that point of inebriation where his vocabulary had reverted to consisting of a very large percentage of four-letter words.

"Tommy," I said, "If I didn't know better, I'd say that you might have been drinking a little bit."

"Of course I've been drinking, you asshole. Did you [hiccup] find my brother yet?"

I noticed that as he said that, Tommy was swaying a little. In the condition he was in, I knew that there was no telling what he might do next. He might collapse on the floor, or he might take a swing at me. I figured either was possible. And honestly, neither would be a big deal, but I thought it best to try to defuse the situation by talking with Tommy about what he obviously wanted to talk about. "Tommy, why don't you sit down? Sit down right here," I said, patting the top of the stool next to me, "and let's talk about your brother."

"What do you [hiccup] know about my brother? Some fucking asshole stole my brother, and I'm going to [hiccup] find him. You know why I've got to find him? 'Cause, you, mister badass [hiccup], and that fucking shithead sheriff's deputy ain't done [hiccup] crap. That's why. And I know where to fucking find him."

"Tommy, that's great you know where to find him. How'd you figure that out?"

"Fuck, mister smartass, it [hiccup] wasn't that fucking hard. I knew the sheriff's boy couldn't figure nothing [hiccup] out, but I thought you might have been able [hiccup] to. It was the dog. That stupid dog is [hiccup] smarter than both of you assholes."

By this time Tommy was swaying further from side to side. I figured he wasn't going to be conscious much longer, and if I wanted to know what he was talking about, I'd better find out quick. "Tommy, what'd you learn from the dog?"

"Every time [hiccup] I'd picked up my brother's dog from the Jug Creek dock, he'd run right back up there as fast as he fucking [hiccup] could. I finally figured out that he [hiccup/gurgle/hiccup/gurgle] was waiting for my brother to come back! Now I know where to go find him."

With that, Tommy lost the battle to keep down his morning's consumption of tequila. Out it came, spewing in a violent, smelly eruption. Fortunately, he had turned away from Jill and me just before it happened. Then, his knees gave out, and he fell, dropping like a stone. He landed hard, splashing in the middle of the pool he had just created, and, with a groan, gently laid his head down to sleep.

Helplessly, I looked over at Shannon behind the bar. She'd been paying attention.

She said, "Y'all go on, and get out of here. We'll take care of Tommy. We've had lots of practice dealing with guys in his condition. We'll take care of him and get him home safe."

"Shannon, are you sure? He's pretty big. Can you handle him?" I asked.

"No. But the guys in the back can. They'll let him sleep for a while, then throw him on the cart we use to move tables, roll him out back, and hose him off. When he starts to come to, we'll drive him home, put him to bed, and keep his keys. He'll know where to find them when he sobers up."

"Damn," I said. "I hate for you to have to deal with this."

"Don't worry about it, honey. It's part of the job description. Y'all get on home."

"Thanks. See ya."

On the drive home, Jill said, "That was pretty awful!"

I agreed. "Yeah, it was. But at least Tommy didn't do anything stupid. I was worried that he might. And in fact, I'm still concerned that once he sobers up, he might still do that."

"What do you mean?" Jill asked.

"I don't really know. I just hope Tommy doesn't go off half-cocked, trying to find his brother, and get into trouble. But I've got to say that his observation about the dog was pretty interesting."

"You think the dog knows something?"

"Probably. Dogs are usually a lot smarter than we are."

Chapter Fifteen

The next morning, in the middle of my second cup of tea, the phone rang. Jill picked it up. After she said hello, I watched her face, trying to get a clue about who was calling. Initially, it gave nothing away, but slowly I saw it dissolve into a grin and noticed a sparkle appear in her eyes. Then I heard her say, "You better watch what you say, you dirty old man, or I'll turn you in to the sheriff. Hold on, and I'll put Jim on."

"Collins, are you propositioning my wife again?" I asked, knowing full well that he and Jill enjoyed their harmless flirtation.

"No. I'm not propositioning your wife *again*," Lieutenant Collins answered. "As far as I can remember, that was the first time I've ever propositioned her. And besides, I don't really consider that to have been a proposition. I prefer to think of it instead as the use of an 'enhanced interrogation technique.' You know, it's important that I keep in practice. But that's not why I called. What are you doing for lunch?"

"I'm open. Jill's got a nail appointment. Where, and when?"

"Let's meet at Woody's, out on the deck. Noon works for me."

"See you there."

"What's up?" Jill asked, once I'd hung up.

"Mike wants to meet for lunch. He didn't say why, but I'd bet it's not because he's trying to be social. Probably wants to update me on the guy we fished up."

A little before noon, I pulled out the trusty bike and leisurely pedaled to Woody's. Upon arrival, I arranged the bike on its kick stand near the "drunkenmost" marker. I then wandered out to the deck, noticing that Collins hadn't arrived yet. I took a seat at a high-top table under a palm tree. It was out of the way and fronted the canal. I figured it would be a good place to have lunch with a cop.

I ordered an unsweetened iced tea. Mike Collins pulled in about five after and slowly ambled toward the deck, checking out the cars in the parking lot as he did. I noticed that today he had heat on his belt. He didn't usually carry.

As he approached the table, I asked, "This table OK?"

"Works for me, as long as one of those damn coconuts doesn't fall and hit me on the head. How you doing?"

"I'm good. But it looks like you're working today," I replied, gesturing toward the Glock on his hip.

"That's pretty observant, for an old fart. Actually, that's why I wanted to talk with you. Have you ordered yet?" he asked.

"Nope. Just this tea. Let's get Chesley over here." I waved at her, and she headed in our direction, her customary smile on her face.

"Good morning, guys," she said. "At least I hope it's a good morning." Turning to Collins she said, "You're not busting Jim again for jaywalking, are you?"

He replied in his best cop voice, "No. He's been moving too damn slowly for that. So I've got him instead for loitering."

Not missing a beat, she replied "Gotcha. Just make sure you let him out in time for 'happy hour.' I need the tip. What can I get you guys?"

We both ordered salads, with seafood on top. I went for ahi tuna; Mike opted for broiled grouper.

"So what's up, Mike?" I asked after she left with our order.

"I hear you went to Key West," he replied.

"Yeah. Is this social?" I asked.

"No. But I do appreciate you getting out of the way so that we could do our jobs."

"That was Jill's idea, not mine," I replied.

"I figured as much. She's the one with the brains. I think we've found something."

"That's great. Fill me in."

"Last night, we busted the pill mill on the island that I was telling you about. We found all kinds of records there, and my boys and girls are out this morning rounding up everyone that was involved. It was a more elaborate scheme than the usual pill mill hustle. In this case, they let it be known in Cape Coral that it was real easy for 'Capers' to come out here to get prescriptions for any pain medications they wanted. But then the guys running the show would photocopy their IDs, and then turn them into new paper, with new photos, for their gophers to use. And they'd duplicate the real prescriptions. The gophers would then go get the pills, making sure not to use the same pharmacies that the patients said they used on their records. They'd then bring the pills back and collect their hundred dollars. A lot of the gophers were ladies who picked crabs over at Buccaneer Crab Company. You can't really blame them. You've got to pick a lot of crabs to earn a hundred bucks. Once the clinic had the pills, then the distribution phase would kick in. And—this is what was cool about this operation—they didn't pay anyone to sell the stuff. They simply used a pyramid marketing scheme. They got the word out to some of the users in town that for every five new users they'd refer in, they'd get one month's pills for free. Business was booming."

"How'd they keep the gophers honest?" I asked.

"That wasn't difficult," Collins told me. "First, the ladies they were dealing with were honest folk to start with. Mostly, they were just good Hispanic ladies trying to make a living and not get deported. Second, they didn't get paid unless they brought back every single pill on the prescription. And finally, we've heard that the one girl who made the mistake of bringing back a couple of short orders disappeared. There were no more short orders after that."

"Guess not," I said. "Any of this tie back to the other disappearances on the island?"

"We're not sure. But I'm betting that it does. There was a lot of money being made, and it was all cash up front. The 'patients' would come in, ask for a fictitious 'Dr. Rodriquez,' be shown back to an exam room, do the transaction—cash for pills—and walk out. Simple. It's always possible that somebody made a mistake, knew too much, or crossed the operation up in some way, and had to suffer the consequences. It's easy to make people disappear out here. One thing we've already learned is that the wedding party had a whole bunch of pills that came from the clinic. So maybe there is something there. We're still looking into that."

By this time our salads had arrived, and we gave them our undivided attention. As we were throwing in the towels, I noticed a small skiff, with one guy and a big yellow dog, heading down the canal toward the bay. I recognized the guy and yelled at him. "Hey, Tommy!"

He heard me, waved, and slowed the boat, turning it sharply to ease over toward where we were sitting.

"Jim, it's good to see you. I need to apologize. I've heard that I wasn't very nice to you and your wife yesterday. I'm sorry about that."

"Apology accepted," I replied. "Where y'all headed? Is that your brother's dog?"

"Yeah. This is Dixie. Smartest damn dog I've ever met. We're going to go out so she can show me where my brother is."

"How's she going to do that? Is she a pointer, or something?" I asked, laughing as I did.

"Jim, this is serious. I don't know exactly how she'll do it. But I know she'll be able to let me know, one way or another. We're going to head up toward the north end of the island and just see what happens. But I'm betting we're going to find my brother."

"Well, good luck," I said. "I hope you find him. But you need to be careful. There are some scary dudes up at Little Bokeelia Island."

"Yeah, I know. But I'm not worried about those Nazis. I've got old Dixie with me. We'll be fine." With that he spun the boat toward the bay and resumed his voyage, adding as he did, "Say hello to Jill."

We watched as they motored south. I swear the dog looked happy and excited to finally be looking for her owner.

"Story, what the fuck is that about? Or do I not want to know?" Collins asked.

I filled him in as best I could, choosing to omit the choicest details of the previous night's encounter at the Legion hall.

"You know, Jim, Pine Island never, ever fails to amaze me," he said at length. "Things out here just 'ain't right.'"

"Mike, I can't argue. But what do you know about the new clinic up on Little Bokeelia?"

"For starters, we don't know that it's a clinic. All we know for sure is that the island and house was sold to a group headed by a Spanish doctor. Taxes are up to date. No complaints from anyone, and no signs of any business solicitations of any sort. We've got no reasons to be concerned about anything. All I know is that some Spaniard owns it, and apparently, he likes his privacy. There's nothing there to concern me."

I looked him in the eyes. He didn't blink, and neither did I. Finally I said, "Mike, in my opinion there *is* something up there for you to be concerned about. You just don't know about it yet. You need to keep an eye on that place."

"You done?" he asked coldly.

"Yep."

We both left twenties on the table and walked out.

Chapter Sixteen

That night Jill and I had dinner with a couple we knew up in Bokeelia. They had been fishing earlier in the day, had brought home a nice mess of snapper, and had called us to join them for dinner. I don't know about you, but for me, nothing beats freshly caught, expertly fried fish. I was delighted they had called. Cheese grits, coleslaw, baked beans, hush puppies, and fried snapper made for a classic cracker feast.

But then it got even better. Our friends, Terry and Patti, lived in a condo that backed up to a large basin, which connected to Jug Creek. The condos had waterside decks and boat docks for owners. After dinner we went outside to our friend's dockside table, where we enjoyed homemade key lime pie and coffee. Fortunately, our friends had lit several citronella candles to keep the sand gnats and mosquitoes away. Finally, we moved on to a round of after-dinner drinks, the girls sharing a wonderful wine while Terry and I slowly savored snifters of a magnificent old rum.

We were having a great time, telling stories and catching up on each other's families, when we noticed gentle swirls in the water just beyond the end of the dock.

"What's that?" I asked.

"Oh, it's just a school of juvenile tarpon. They're here just about every night. I guess this must be a nursery area, or something. And it probably doesn't hurt that I throw all my excess white bait out there when I come in from fishing. They seem to like it. They also seem to like the flies that I've been pitching at them with my fly rod. That is a lot of fun."

"I bet it is," I agreed.

Then Terry said, "But tarpon aren't the only thing you can catch off the dock. I know it's hard to believe but there are goliath grouper that live underneath it. I swear that one of them is well over a hundred pounds. I've tried to catch him, but he's torn up all my stuff. I've thought about putting a fourteen aught shark hook on some cable, and tying it off on a dock piling, just to see if I can get the best of him. But I've thought better of that. Even if I caught him, and even if he didn't pull down the dock, I'd have to turn him loose. It's just not worth the effort."

"I hear you. But it's amazing you've got them in here. How deep's the water under the dock?"

"You know it's funny, but its only eight feet. I guess they just like the structure down there."

About then we noticed that the tarpon were becoming more active. Not only were they swirling, but now they were broaching. We could see the fishes' dorsal fins, with their characteristic threads trailing behind. Terry and I quietly watched the show, sipping our drinks while the ladies chatted happily about the latest exploits of their obviously very special grandchildren. I was just thinking about asking my friend if I could try his fly rod when we noticed a boat slowly moving under the bridge that spanned Jug Creek. It turned, and we could tell, as we were seeing both red and green lights on its bow, that it was heading directly toward us. That wasn't unusual, given that the condo complex has multiple docks for owners. However, what was different was the big yellow dog on the boat's bow, barking its fool head off.

As the boat approached, Terry finally recognized that it was his neighbor's boat and that his neighbor and wife were on board, along with the dog. It had taken him a while to put it all together as his neighbors don't own a dog.

"Hey, Jack," Terry yelled. "When did you get a dog?"

"About ten minutes ago," Jack responded. "The damn fool thing was out in the middle of the mangroves, right in the middle of nowhere, just swimming up Jug Creek to beat the band. It looked to us like he must have had somewhere important to go. As soon as he saw us he started barking like crazy. We pulled him on board. I reckon that if we hadn't, a gator or a shark would have gotten him by now. And he's been barking ever since. It's like he's trying to tell us something. I sure do wish I could understand him. Do y'all know who he belongs to?"

My friend answered that he didn't have a clue. But I said that I might, and then I spoke to the dog. "Dixie, Dixie, you hush."

The dog stopped barking, tilted its head to the side, looked at me with a questioning look as if trying to remember where it knew me from, and then quietly whined. I knew the dog was asking me for help.

"Oh, shit!" I said. "I know this dog. I'm pretty sure it belongs to Tommy's brother. Tommy's a friend of mine down in Saint James. I saw her and Tommy onboard a boat at noon today. They were heading up this way, trying to locate Tommy's brother, who's gone missing. This doesn't look good. I think we better call the sheriff."

The neighbor asked, "You're going to call the sheriff over a dog?"

I answered, "Look, I'm betting that you finding that dog means that Tommy's now missing, too. His brother has been missing for a week. There is something going on out here, and it's not good. We need the sheriff, and we need him now."

Terry said, "Y'all tie up, and then bring the dog on over to my place. I'm going to go on in and make the call."

I said, "Ask for Lieutenant Mike Collins, and tell him that Jim Story said to get his ass out here as quickly as he can."

The ladies had already run over to where the boat was going to dock and were talking to Dixie to try to calm her down. I knew they were worried about her. And I was worried, too. I was also worried about Tommy—and about his brother.

Chapter Seventeen

Ten minutes after the call, the first deputies were on scene, their flashing blue lights illuminating the normally tranquil complex. They secured the area, but beyond that, they didn't seem to know what to do. I suspect that they had not been trained on how to interrogate a dog.

Thirty minutes later, Lieutenant Collins pulled up in his SUV. He saw us standing down by the dock and ambled our way. He still had the Glock on his hip. He looked tired.

I expected him to lay into me, accusing me of once again doing my best to uphold Pine Island's reputation for wackiness. But tonight he surprised me. "Jim. Jill," he greeted us quietly.

I introduced him to our friends and to the neighbors who had found the dog.

"Where's the dog?" he asked.

"Inside," Terry said.

"Let's go," Mike said.

We walked through the sliding glass door into the family room of the condo. The first thing we noticed was the dog snoring on the couch. Apparently, her swim had worn her out.

We found places to sit, trying to not disturb the dog's slumber. As soon as we were sitting, Mike asked the neighbors to tell him what had transpired. He asked them to show him on a chart exactly where they had come across the dog. Next, he asked me what I knew. I gave him the whole story about Tommy, and Tommy's brother, and Tommy's brother's dog. I told him about the dog hanging out at, and returning to, Jug Creek Marina. And I reminded him of us meeting Tommy and Dixie at Woody's earlier in the day.

Then Mike quietly said, "OK. I've got a couple of our boats heading this way. They'll put in at the marina, and we'll go out to search. It's tough to find anything in the dark, though. But we'll keep at it all night. In the morning, if we haven't found him, we'll change crews, and keep searching until we do. We'll get the word out to the Coast Guard. They'll make sure all boaters in the area are on the lookout for any sign of either Tommy or the boat. Now, Jim, let me ask you something. Did Tommy have a drinking problem?"

I knew what Lieutenant Collins was thinking, and I hated to have to confirm that Tommy had been drinking recently; he'd been drinking a lot.

"Mike, he's been drinking heavily ever since his brother disappeared. He passed out the other night down at the Legion. I think he's been worried to death about his brother. But I don't think that's what happened to him."

"Jim, I appreciate your opinion. But my guess is that Tommy probably got frustrated out on the boat, got thirsty, got drunk, fell overboard, and drowned. Then, the dog decided to swim for home. I'm betting we'll find the boat, but we won't find Tommy. At least, not for a while. He'll float in about a week."

"Mike," I replied. "I don't think that's what happened. First, Tommy's a good boater, and I'd bet he knows to not drink out on the water. And second, there's something going on at that clinic on Little Bokeelia, and that has something to do with whatever has happened to Tommy—and to his brother."

"You got any evidence?" Mike asked.

"No."

"I didn't think so," Mike responded. "But we'll stop by there, just to see if they know anything."

As we spoke, the dog started to wake up. She opened her eyes and looked around the room with her head still on the cushions. Then, apparently not seeing what, or whom, she wanted to see, she jumped off the couch and bounded over to the sliding glass doors.

"I think she's got to go," Jill said. "You want me to let her out?"

"No. I wouldn't let her out without a leash. I suspect that if you do, she'll jump right back in the water and start swimming over to the marina," I said.

Terry said "Wait a minute." He disappeared into a side room, and came back out, holding what looked to be a twenty-foot section of three-eighths-inch dock line. "This is all I've got, but tie this on to her."

Jill put one end through the ring on her collar, pulled that through the dock line's looped end, and then pulled it tight.

Holding tightly to the line's other end, she slid open the glass doors, and let the dog step outside. The rest of us followed.

"Mike, are you going to take the dog with you on one of your boats?"

"No. Policy says that I can't do that. We'll have some of our own body-sniffing dogs onboard, and they might not get along with Dixie."

"You got any objections to us taking her out on our boat and searching on our own?" I asked.

"Nope. Just stay out of our way, and don't go messing around out at Little Bokeelia. We'll take care of that place."

"OK. But I'm telling you, those guys have something to do with this."

Before Mike could reply, his radio barked, and I could hear that the search boats were in the water at Jug Creek Marina. Mike asked one of them to head our way to pick him up. Seconds later we heard twin outboards revving up, followed shortly by the sight of a fast-moving boat sliding around the point. It headed our way with a strong searchlight sweeping the water from side to side. Behind that, we could see a matching inflatable slowly easing along the Jug Creek shoreline, its searchlight carefully illuminating the mangroves, then sweeping out to the middle of the channel. The boat eased forward a few feet and repeated the pattern. It was going to be a long night. I hoped that Tommy was going to be OK.

We searched all night—our friends, Jill, me and Dixie. The dog had clearly been trying to help, using her nose to try to catch a scent. But she hadn't. Occasionally she'd bark, but when she did, she'd bark just once. Then she'd listen, as if she were expecting to hear a call for help. However, she didn't appear to have heard that, either. It had been a long night for the humans onboard, and I think it had been a long night for Dixie, too.

Mike had given us a handheld radio, tuned to the channel that the deputies were using. We listened as they talked back and forth. They were doing a very professional job. However, nobody had found anything. We were about ready to give up and head back to the condo for some breakfast, but just as the sun came up, a little after six thirty, we heard the radio crackle.

"Sixty-three, sixty-three, this is boat two. Come back."

"Two, sixty-three. What's up?"

"I think we've found the missing boat. The numbers match."

"Anyone onboard?"

"Nobody's onboard."

"OK. Where are you?"

"A little north of Patricio."

"I'm on the way."

And so were we. During the radio transmission, the dog's ears had picked up, as if she were listening to the conversation. I'd guess that she didn't have a clue about what was said, but when we throttled up to head toward Patricio Island, there was no doubt that she knew something was up. She barked happily, jumped up to the bow, and stuck her nose out as far ahead of the boat as she could without risking being bounced off. I'm sure she was expecting to be able to shortly rendezvous with Tommy and his brother. The only time I noticed her excitement wane was when we flew by Little Bokeelia. Then she glared in that direction, growled softly, and bared her teeth. It was clear that there was something over there that she didn't like.

As we came out of the channel, we could see Mike's boat ahead of us. We followed in its wake. The inflatable was faster, but it wasn't far to Patricio. We pulled in shortly after Mike. There was no doubt that the deputies had found Tommy's boat—and no doubt that Tommy wasn't onboard.

We heard Lieutenant Collins ask the deputies in the other boat as we arrived, "What'd you find?"

"Not much," the senior deputy answered. "No sign of a struggle. No blood. Nothing's broken. But there's an empty Smirnoff bottle on the floor."

With that Mike looked over at me, and shrugged. It was a shrug full of meaning. A shrug that told me that this is what he had expected to find, that he was sorry that it had turned out like this, and that he had seen this kind of thing far too many times. He really looked tired now. I couldn't help but notice that Dixie looked tired, too. She was whining.

"OK," Mike said to the other officers. "Y'all put your anchor out, mark the spot on your GPS, and tie the boat up to yours. I'll get our other guys out here to start searching the area, and I'll get a crime scene unit, too."

Then he turned to us, and said, "Jim, there's nothing else y'all can do now. Why don't you head on in?" He'd asked, but I knew that it was really a directive for us to get out of his hair.

"OK, Mike. Give me a call later."

Chapter Eighteen

Jill and I went home. Our friends kept the dog. We slept most of the day and woke up a little before four o'clock. Grumpily, we worked our ways downstairs. We weren't sure whether to have some coffee or to fix a drink. Staying up all night and sleeping all day sure messes you up. We opted for coffee.

We went close to an hour without speaking, just enjoying the taste of the coffee and the stimulant it contained. Eventually, the caffeine started to reset our clocks, and we began to focus on what we would do for the rest of the day.

"Babe, how are you feeling?" I asked.

She rolled her eyes at me, and mumbled something. I think she said that she was peachy. I didn't buy it, but at least she had responded. I thought that was a positive sign. So I pressed on.

"What are we going to do tonight?" I asked.

"Whatever we do, it better not having anything to do with a damn boat!" was Jill's answer.

"Shoot! And I was really looking forward to taking the *Pulapanga* over to Doc Ford's tonight," I joked.

This time she didn't even bother to reply. The look she gave me said it all.

"OK, OK," I said. "No Doc Ford's. I'm OK with that. Why don't we just rest up here for a while? A little later we can get cleaned up and go down to Woody's for dinner. You OK with that?"

"Yeah."

A little after seven, we slowly drove to Woody's. It took us three minutes. As we walked in, we noticed there was a pretty good crowd. I guessed it was due to the guitar player in the corner. However, right then we weren't in the mood for music. We found a table toward the back.

We sat down, and one of the servers headed our way. It was a new girl; we didn't recognize her. She quickly took our drink orders, left menus, and went away to fetch the refreshments. That was all good.

She came back with our drinks in a few minutes, and we quietly set about emptying our glasses. Our internal clocks were still all messed up, but the drinks were helping to recalibrate us. I guessed that after another couple of rounds, we'd be roughly in the correct time zone.

Ten minutes later, the waitress showed up to see if we were ready to order food or another round of drinks. We took her up on both. As she was leaving, I asked her to tell Adam that I wanted to talk with him. From the look on her face, I didn't think she was used to telling Adam anything. I laughed and assured her that it would be all right.

Adam brought our next round to the table. As he walked up he said, "Hey, guys. How are y'all doing? Lisa said that you wanted to see me. Did she screw up something again?"

Jill spoke up, "Adam, you let that little girl alone. She's doing a fine job. Another night or two, and she'll be a pro. I like her."

"That's good to hear," Adam replied. "Now what's up?"

"Adam, I need to ask you a question. Can you sit down for a minute?" I said.

"Just for a minute—the bar's pretty busy," he said as he slid onto a stool next to Jill.

"Have you heard about Tommy going missing?" I asked.

"Yeah. Everybody's talking about that," Adam replied. "That's too bad. I heard he got drunk and fell overboard."

"That's what I want to ask you about," I said. "Did you ever know Tommy to drink vodka?"

"No. He wouldn't touch the stuff. He told me one night that he'd gotten sick on it, back when he was a teenager, and now he couldn't stand the thought of drinking it. I've never known him to drink it. Why?"

"Just curious. It looks like business is pretty good."

"Yeah, it's been better this year than last. I guess the economy's picking up. I'm thinking we're going to stay open all summer."

"I hope so. We need a place to go get out of the house," Jill responded.

Adam laughed and asked, "Can I get you guys anything?"

"No. We're good. You better get back to the bar."

When he'd gone, Jill looked at me and said, "You thinking what I'm thinking?"

I looked at her and replied, "Tommy didn't fall out of that damn boat."

Chapter Nineteen

We finished eating. The food was delicious, just like always at Woody's. We could have just stayed, enjoyed the music, had a few more drinks, and then gone home. That would have been the way we normally would have played the evening. However, we'd slept all day and were still feeling kind of restless. We needed to keep going for a while.

"What'd you think about going down to the Legion for a while?" I asked. "I think they're playing 'Show Me the Money' tonight."

"That sounds like fun. Let's go."

The Legion's parking lot was almost full. "Show Me the Money" was sort of a cross between poker and bingo, and it was played in the bar area. The bottom line was that it cost a dollar per set of cards to play each round. People could buy as many card sets as they liked. That doesn't sound like much, but there would usually be twenty rounds each evening. So playing two sets of cards all evening could cost you forty bucks. That's not exactly cheap for Saint James City. The good news was that the Legion paid out 80 percent of each hand. Therefore, there was a good chance you could recoup most of your card costs before the evening was through. And the beer was cheap. So all in all, it was not a bad way to spend some time.

We walked into the bar, found a couple of empty stools, and spent a couple of minutes exchanging greetings with the others who were sitting around the bar. It was, after all, Saint James City. And, as was customary, Jill knew many more folks there than I did. While she was making her way around the bar, hugging all the ladies and catching up, I ordered the drinks and got our first set of cards.

The ladies who ran the game didn't let any grass grow. To get the twenty games in, they needed to play a round every six minutes. Furthermore, during that time they had to satisfy everyone's need to buy or exchange card sets; play the game; pay out the winnings; and allow a couple of minutes to reshuffle the deck for the next game. They kept it moving.

I had actually played our first three rounds before Jill completed her circumnavigation of the huge bar—but I hadn't won. In fact, I hadn't even come close. I explained that to Jill as she perched on her stool. Then I quietly accepted her good-natured ribbing. She assured me that with her now in the game, our luck was sure to change. When the lady came around selling cards for the next round, she turned in the losers that I had been playing and drew two new hands. And sure enough, it took only six cards being drawn from the deck before she yelled, "Show me the money!" She'd won thirty-eight bucks. I knew I'd be hearing about that for a long time to come.

The game progressed quickly. As the evening moved on, the good-natured crowd gradually became more animated, with the winners coming in for their share of razzing from the losers. It was fun. Then, as the game neared its end, the room's most vocal, and most humorous, loser brought the house down when he loudly threatened to complain to the area's very well-known contingency-compensated law firm. The joke was perfectly timed. Everyone laughed. Finally, when the dealing was done, we had won two rounds and were up a few bucks, even after netting out the cost of our beverages.

As the crowd drifted out, I finally got the opportunity that I had been waiting for all evening. "Shannon, did you hear about Tommy?"

"Yeah. That is terrible," she responded. "I knew he'd been drinking a lot, but I never thought that he'd get drunk and fall out of his boat. From what I knew, he was always careful when he was on the water. He even told me one time that he never, ever drank when he was on a boat. He said that the water was just too hostile an environment to take that kind of chance."

"I hear you. That's my rule, too. I never start drinking until my feet are on dry land. But the Sheriff says that they found an empty vodka bottle on Tommy's boat. So I guess he must have broken his rule."

"Jim, that can't be right!" she exclaimed. "There is absolutely no way that he would have gotten drunk on vodka. He hated the stuff. He wouldn't touch it. He didn't care if it was plain, flavored, cheap, expensive, mixed in a drink, whatever. Apparently, the first time he got drunk back in high school, he'd been drinking Smirnoff. He said he was sick for over twenty-four hours. It was a story that all the regulars in here knew. They'd always kid him about it and offer to buy him a vodka martini. It would just piss him off."

"Shannon, the bottle they found was a Smirnoff bottle," I told her.

"There is no way. You can take my word for it—Tommy didn't fall out of his boat after drinking a bottle of Smirnoff. Y'all want another round?"

At this point, Jill spoke up, "No, we'd better not. I need to get this old guy home before he blows all my winnings."

Shannon laughed, and I pretended to be upset, but we walked out of the Legion holding hands—two old farts still deeply in love.

Chapter Twenty

"Good morning, Jim."

"Mike," I replied. "Have you caught up on your sleep yet?"

"In my business, you never catch up on your sleep. You know the old saying about nothing good happening after midnight? Well, that's the story of my life. Very few folks show the courtesy anymore to get murdered during bankers' hours. Oh, shit. I forgot that you used to be a banker, Jim. Sorry."

From the sarcasm in his voice I knew that Lieutenant Collins was enjoying pulling my leg. I also figured that he was still a little bit out of sorts, not having fully recovered from a night spent on the sound batting mosquitoes and slapping at sand gnats. And I figured that what I was getting ready to tell him would make him even more out of sorts.

"Mike, you need to get yourself a better class of clients. Have you thought about transferring down to Naples?"

"Shit," he replied. "Those folks down there are just as crazy. The only difference is that they can afford better lawyers. And that would just end up making my job even harder. What's up?"

"Have you found Tommy yet?" I asked.

"No. We've still got a boat out looking, but I really don't expect that he'll float for another couple of days."

"Mike," I said. "Tommy didn't get drunk and fall out of his boat."

For once, he didn't say anything. I waited for almost a minute. Finally, I asked, "You still there?"

"Story," he began. I had learned that when he called me by my last name that he was probably pissed. That didn't surprise me. "Why the fuck don't you think that's what happened?"

"Tommy didn't drink vodka."

"Maybe that's all he had."

"Nope. Everyone in town's telling me that he absolutely hated the stuff. You couldn't get him to drink it, even if his life depended on it. I think that somebody either grabbed him or killed him and then put that bottle in the boat to make it look like he got drunk and fell overboard. But he didn't fall out of his boat. In my opinion, somebody set you up."

I could hear Collins let out a deep sigh. I guessed he was trying to control his blood pressure and hoped that he wasn't about to get a migraine. Finally he spoke. "Story, before you came to town, my life used to be so simple. All I had to do was figure out who owed whom. Or whose spouse was off the reservation. Put the pieces together and then lock the culprits up. But not anymore. Now, every time I turn around, I have to deal with some convoluted mess that you're in the middle of. I'm starting to think that the best thing I could do would be to run your ass out of town. Jill could stay, though."

"Mike, I'm just trying to help," I reminded him.

"Yeah, I know. So, who do you think did it? You got that figured out, too?"

"I've got no proof. You know that. But my guess would be that it has something to do with that Spanish doctor on Little Bokeelia and those Nazis who patrol his island. I suspect that Tommy and the dog went to the island to look for his brother. From there, I don't know what happened. Maybe they drowned him. Or maybe they've still got him. But if I were you, I'd go raid the place as soon as I could."

"Great idea, Story," he said sarcastically. "That's just what I'm going to do. I'll go talk to a judge right now, and ask him to sign a search warrant. When he wants to know why I think I'm entitled to violate the doctor's constitutional rights against an unreasonable search, I'll explain that it's because Jim Story suspects that the doctor might be up to something. I'm sure that will be more than enough to light a fire under any of the judges at the courthouse."

"Cute. What *are* you going to do?" I asked.

"I will look into the guy and see what I can find. At the very least I can take a look at the property transaction to see if there was anything squirrelly about that. And I'll see if Interpol has anything on the guy. But if I remember correctly, you've got some contacts in Spain. If I get you his name, you think you could have one of your Spanish friends tell us what they know about the guy?"

"Sure. That worked out last time. Who knows? Maybe lightning will strike twice."

"I'll be in touch."

Chapter Twenty-One

Mike Collins called back a half hour later. He had information about who had purchased the island. I immediately called one of my Spanish contacts.

"Arantxa, how are you?"

I had called Arantxa Garcia-Myer on her cell phone. She was a Spaniard who worked for the huge global bank I had worked for before I retired. She was also a friend. She was responsible for documenting policies and procedures in the American portion of the organization. She was a very busy lady. I had called her cell phone because she traveled constantly and was never in her New York office. It was always interesting, when talking with her, to find out where she was. I sometimes joked with her that she was like a real-life version of that old computer game, "Where in the World is Carmen Sandiego?"

"Jim! It is so good to hear from you. We all miss you so much," she told me.

"Thanks," I replied. "We miss you, too. Arantxa, before we go any further, I've got to ask, where in the world are you today?"

She laughed. "I'm sitting in the Birmingham airport, on my way to Houston. Two days there, and then back to New York. Next week I'm heading to Madrid for a couple of weeks. I'm so excited. You and Jill want to come home with me?"

Now, it was my turn to laugh. "Arantxa, you know that we don't travel much anymore. Just going off island to Fort Myers is an exciting trip for us. But that's not why I called."

"No. I didn't think so. Is something wrong?" Arantxa asked.

The last time I had called her out of the blue, something had most definitely been wrong. I had called her to ask for her help in finding out why our friend Jorge Hernandez had been killed. Eventually, she had been able to provide information from Spain that was the key to unraveling that mystery.

"Unfortunately, there is something wrong. But thankfully, this time it doesn't involve anyone you know. However, I think there may be a connection back to Spain. That's why I called you."

"Jim, I thought you had retired to go fishing and to enjoy a quiet and peaceful life. But instead, every time you call, someone has been killed, and you have to find out who did it. I think you've retired to a very dangerous place. Maybe you need to move back to Alabama. I think you would be much safer there."

"I doubt that," I joked. "You know how big a Gators fan Jill is. When we lived up there, I was always worried that she'd start running her mouth about how great the Gators were. If she'd done that in front of the wrong 'Bammer' or 'Aube,' there's no telling what might have happened. I think it's a good thing we left when we did."

"They do like the football," she agreed. "And the folks in Texas do, too. But, Jim, that's not why you called. How may I be of assistance?"

I told her about Tommy, his brother, the dog, the guards, the Spanish doctor, and his clients. When I had finished, I asked her thoughts on the best way to get information on the doctor.

"Jim, you remember Juan Carlos Fernandez? He is responsible in the bank for all Credit and Risk in the United States. I think he might be the best person for you to ask. If the doctor has any kind of credit record, either here or in Spain, Juan Carlos could find out. And you know how those Credit guys are. Their decisions are about a lot more than just cash flow and collateral. For them, character ranks equally. If the doctor ever tried to borrow money, they'll be able to tell you all there is to know about him. Why don't you give Juan Carlos a call?" she suggested.

"That sounds like a good idea. Do you have his number?" I asked.

"Give me a second."

She put me on hold but was soon back on the line to give me his number. Then she said, "Jim, if he can't help you, or if you need any other information, please let me know. Being a detective is fun."

I thanked her, promised to keep her updated, told her to enjoy her trip home, and hung up.

I called the number Arantxa had provided.

"Juan Carlos Fernandez's office. This is Shirley. How may I help you?" came the reply.

One of the things I had enjoyed, after the Spanish bank bought the Alabama-based banking company for which I had previously worked, was the blending of accents you would encounter throughout the day. It took a while before we Americans could decipher the Spaniards' heavily accented, but perfectly translated, English. And, I'm sure it was equally frustrating for them to work their ways through the slow drawls of those of us from a Southern background.

Shirley, I remembered, spoke with one of the most pure Southern drawls in the bank. I always thought that it was beautiful, a classic example of Old Alabama diction. I'm sure it drove the quick-speaking Spaniards crazy, but they tolerated it happily because of Shirley's unequaled administrative competence. She knew all there was to know about how the bank really operated and who you needed to talk with when something needed to be fixed. She was an invaluable resource for Juan Carlos. I wasn't surprised that she was still on his team.

"Shirley, this is Jim Story. How are you?"

"Jim Story! It is so good to hear from you. How are you and Jill?"

Shirley and I had known each other for years. We spent twenty minutes catching up. It was great talking with her and finding out how she was doing. We also discussed her husband, her kids, and her grandkids. Finally, I got around to asking her if Juan Carlos was available.

"No, Jim. Today's Credit Committee day. He'll be in Committee all day, and probably well into the evening. Can he get back to you tomorrow?"

As an ex-banker, I certainly remembered Credit Committee days. In a well-run bank, there was absolutely nothing more important than the process of formally ratifying decisions to lend significant amounts of money. I knew that I had zero chance of getting through to Juan Carlos that day. So I told Shirley, "Yes, that will be fine. Just ask him to give me a call when he has a moment."

She said that she would.

Chapter Twenty-Two

At eight thirty the next morning, the house phone rang. I read in the caller ID that the call was made from a 205 area code. I knew that was the code for Birmingham, Alabama. I also remembered that, due to the time zone difference, it was seven thirty in the morning there. That would be early for most bankers to be calling—and very, very, very early for most Spanish bankers. However, I remembered that Juan Carlos, unlike many of his countrymen, was always in the bank early.

"Hello," I answered.

"Jim, this is Juan Carlos. How are you?" I immediately recognized his pleasant, professional, and slightly accented voice. After the bank had been sold, one of the first things we learned about out new Spanish bosses was that they were much, much better educated than we Americans. And I have always suspected that Juan Carlos probably had the best education of them all. However, unlike some of the Spaniards we interacted with, he never appeared to have the need to use that to position himself as superior. Rather, when you spoke with him, you always felt that he was genuinely listening to, and carefully evaluating the merits of, whatever arguments you were making. And even more importantly, you always felt that he would be willing to adopt your position and even go to bat for it, if he recognized that it had merit. He was one of the good guys.

"Juan Carlos! I am doing great. And how are you?"

"Better now that the economy is beginning to turn around. The last four years have been terrible for those of us in Credit. Just about every real estate loan on the books has either been written off or restructured. Now, thankfully, things are beginning to turn around. At least they are here. In Spain, things are still not improving. I'm just praying that they don't want me to move back there to deal with that mess. If they call, I'm going to quit, move to Florida, and get you to take me fishing."

I laughed, but I knew the stress that he had been under. The Spanish bank had invested billions of dollars to buy the US bank and had then had to put in multiples of that amount to recapitalize it as the economy tanked. Management in Spain had not been happy. Juan Carlos was the guy they had sent to deal with the mess in the loan portfolio; he was one of their brightest. In his position, having been sent to clean up a problem, he could well have afforded to act like an asshole. That's probably how most would have expected him to act. However, that was not his style. He was a professional and a gentleman. He was tough, but at the same time, he was patient and a genuinely nice person. Unfortunately, in the financial industry, that's not common. Those who worked with him respected and liked him.

"Fishing's great," I said. "Come on down, and I'll put you on some tarpon that will make you forget every problem you've ever had!"

He laughed. "Don't tempt me. Don't tempt me. If I could, I'd leave right now. But, unfortunately, I can't. Now, Jim, how may I help you?"

I knew that I'd wasted enough of his time, so I quickly explained why I had called. "Juan Carlos, I'm looking for information about Dr. Ricardo Areola Fuentes. He, or rather a group he is associated with, purchased a large island down here about a year ago. The group is called Andalusia Properties. According to the tax records, it paid twenty-two million US dollars. Then someone spent more, building some kind of medical clinic on the island. Now they guard it like it's a military base. Periodically, folks come and go—some of whom look sick, some not so much. But everything is kept extremely quiet. No one mixes or even talks with the locals. It's real strange. Personally, I'm convinced that something bad is going on, and that it somehow relates to the disappearance of a number of people on the island, some of whom are friends of mine. So if you can get any information about Dr. Areola, I'd very much appreciate it."

"Jim, I have friends in Spain who may be able to help. Even if Dr. Areola is not known to our bank, someone there will know someone who knows him. Can you give me three or four days?" he replied.

"Juan Carlos, I know you will do what you can. But the life of a good friend of mine may well depend upon how quickly you can get information on this guy. I may not have three or four days to wait. I hate to sound dramatic, and I know it's always bad form to try to pressure a credit guy, but this may truly be a matter of life or death!" I told him.

"I will do what I can do."

"I know you will. Thank you."

Chapter Twenty-Three

Now what? The day was young.

"Hey, babe," I said to Jill. "You want to go fishing? The weather's great, and the tide's coming in. It should be a fabulous day."

"You know, your idea of great weather and mine don't always line up. Anytime it's going to be over ninety degrees, like it's going to be today, I don't call that great—I call that hot. I think I'll pass. Why don't you call Kenny and see if he wants to go with you?"

"I'd rather go fishing with you."

"Yeah, and I'd rather go shopping and stay cool. Just call Kenny."

A little while later, I picked up the phone and dialed. "Kenny, this is Jim. You want to go try to catch some redfish in a little bit?"

"Sure. When do you want to leave?"

"I'll pick you up at ten. The tide's going to be high a little after one. I figure it'll be about right for fishing the bushes for a couple of hours."

"What are we going to do for bait?" Kenny asked.

"I'll just throw the net out for some pinfish," I said. "Shouldn't take more than a couple of minutes to have all we need."

Kenny replied, "Sounds good to me. See you in a while."

I told Jill about the plan, and then I told her I was going to go fish the north end of the island. Probably somewhere near Patricio Island.

She looked at me kind of funny and said, "Kind of a long way to go just to try to catch a redfish, isn't it? Aren't there plenty of those near the mouth of our canal?"

"Yeah. But I've been wanting to fish the mangroves up there. I've heard lots of good things about that area."

"It wouldn't have anything to do with you looking for Tommy's body, would it?" Jill asked.

"I'll keep my eyes open, "I assured her. "But I don't really think that we'll find Tommy's body floating in the sound."

"Just promise me," she said, "that whatever y'all do, you won't go messing with those goons on Little Bokeelia."

"OK. But if we don't come home by dark, that would be where I would start looking, if I were you."

I didn't like the look she gave me.

Then she said, "Give me a call on the phone before you start for home, just so I'll know when to expect you. And please, you and Kenny try to stay out of trouble."

I started to say something smart in response but thought better of that. Instead, I just looked her in the eyes and nodded.

In the heat of the summer, redfish get lazy. I guess the hot water saps all their energy. The only time you can catch one feeding away from the mangroves is very early in the morning.

There's a saying down here that in the summer, once the sun comes up over the mangroves, you're wasting your time trying to catch a redfish on anything that moves. About the only thing that works during the heat of the day is throwing a piece of cut bait as far up under the shade of a mangrove tree as you can get it, when the tide is high. Live bait usually won't work because that requires the redfish to make an effort to pursue the bait as it attempts to escape. Usually, we used pinfish for bait and cut them in two. Redfish don't have great vision, but their sense of smell is excellent; they get excited about the scent of blood in the water. That's how we planned to fish that day.

Kenny and I stopped on a grass flat a little outside the mouth of our canal, put down the shallow-water anchor, and began to throw little chum balls into the water. I buy chum in dried, powdered form. When I'm ready to use it, I pour a little into a bucket, moisten it with salt water, roll it into balls, and slowly throw a few into the water, slightly up-current of where I plan to cast my bait net. If I'm fishing for white bait, I need to wait until I see them schooling near the surface. However, this is not the case for pinfish. You can find pinfish on just about any grass flat in the sound, but to get them to congregate, it's good to encourage them with a little chum. If you take a couple of minutes to let them discover where the chum is located, you shouldn't need to throw your net more than just a couple of times to catch all you will need to fish. And that's what happened.

"All right, Captain," Kenny said. "Where're you going to take us?"

"I was thinking we'd head up to the north end of the sound. I've heard good things about fishing up there."

"Shit, Jim. That's a long way to run just to catch some redfish. You sure you want to do that?"

"Yeah, I do. Look, Kenny, the last time you took me fishing, you guaranteed me that I'd catch a redfish within ten minutes. And what happened?" I asked.

"Near as I remember, it only took you five minutes to have one in the boat. A twenty-four incher, if I recall."

"Actually, it took eight minutes. But it was a nice fish. So anyway, the pressure's on me now. I've got to make sure you catch some fish, and I've heard they're really biting up there. And besides, I don't think the red tide is quite as bad there. It'll probably be worth the time to run up to the north end."

"This wouldn't have anything to do with looking for Tommy, would it?" Kenny asked.

Feigning shock, I said, "Kenny! I'm surprised that you would think that of me. Can I help it that the fish are reported to be hanging out around Little Bokeelia Island?"

Chapter Twenty-Four

As soon as we had cleared the restricted manatee speed zones I pushed the engine's throttle forward. The *Pulapanga* responded, quickly and lightly leaping up onto a plane, sliding across the top of the glassy water, heading north. We didn't encounter much traffic, only a couple of large trawlers working up the channel, probably returning from the Keys or the Bahamas and heading home. They cast out large wakes, but as we were running slightly east of the channel, we were able to slide over them without having to slow. Forty-five minutes later, I dropped the boat off plane and poked in toward the mangrove shoreline south of Little Bokeelia. It really did look like a good place to fish. It also looked like a good place from which to scope out what was happening on the doctor's island.

We cut up some nice pinfish and pitched them up in the shade with minimal drama. Fishing like this, it was not unusual to catch more mangrove limbs than fish. Honestly, it was not my favorite way to go angling. At least not up until the moment when a nice-sized redfish decides to hook itself on the end of my line. Redfish, also called red drum, are the brutes of inshore fishing in Florida. They are strong and sturdily built. The slot size for a fish you can keep is between eighteen and twenty-seven inches. The catch limit is one per angler. However, it's not uncommon to catch a red that is well over thirty inches in length. A fish like that is called a bull red. That name tells you a lot about how hard a fish that size will fight.

It didn't take long for us to have action. Kenny, as usual, was trying to entice the fish to his offerings by talking to them.

"Here, fishy, fishy, fishy!" Kenny purred.

I didn't put much stock in that stuff, but it wasn't more than two minutes later when his cork started to move. It moved slowly but steadily, headed further up under the mangroves. Because of the way it was behaving, you could tell that it wasn't a little Mangrove Snapper messing with the bait. But Kenny was patient, trying to make sure that the fish had plenty of time to taste the bait and get it well into its mouth. Finally, when he couldn't wait any longer if he wanted to have a chance to keep the fish out of the mangrove roots, he set the hook and leaned back against the fish. It was a good hookup. His drag was set tight to keep the fish out of the roots, and shortly he was able to drag the red out from under the trees. But we couldn't get a good look at how big it was because, even though the water was shallow, it was stained dark by tannin. It took a couple more minutes of fighting before Kenny was finally able to bring the fish to the boat. I scooped it up in the landing net, coming in from behind to make sure I didn't knock it off the hook. It was a big fish, just below the upper slot limit, a keeper. It went into the live well.

Kenny, as was his style, was excited. "Whooeee! Whooeee! Wow! What a fish. Jim, you did good."

"So the pressure's off, right?"

"You bet. I figured you didn't have a clue about where to catch a fish up here. But instead, what do you do? You come all the way up here, and then drive right up to a tree that's crawling with reds. I'm impressed! Maybe you do know what you're doing."

"You know better than that," I answered. "It was just dumb luck—the same kind of luck you needed to be able to land that fish."

"Luck, my ass. That was skill, boy. Now let's try to catch another one."

It didn't take long for Kenny to score again. This time it was a smaller, twenty-inch fish. Then a twenty-four-inch fish. That one went into the box, and we released the smaller fish that was already there. With all that action, I was beginning to get frustrated that I hadn't caught anything, but finally I hooked a fifteen-incher. We couldn't keep it, but at least it was something. Then I landed a thirty-one-inch monster. It was by far the best day of redfish fishing that I had ever enjoyed. It was a good thing that our surveillance of the island didn't require us to be quiet. We were hooting, and hollering to beat the band. Truthfully, for a while we completely forgot about the island.

But our attention to it was brought back when a helicopter landed on the island's landing pad. We were too far away to see much about the person who got out. But it was someone in a wheelchair. I'd guess a new patient for the clinic. As soon as this person was wheeled away, and into the main house, the chopper took off- and headed northeast. I figured it was going back to Punta Gorda.

"Kenny," I said. "We've got our limit in the box. What would you say if we were to try our luck over by the south shore of that island?"

"There's no mangroves there."

"No, there's not, and we probably won't catch any fish there, but the view's a lot better."

"Let's go."

Chapter Twenty-Five

Little Bokeelia Island was shaped roughly like the letter Y, written in cursive by someone who is right-handed. The westernmost arm was positioned so that it aimed roughly toward the northeast, whereas the other arm curved around to the east. We were fishing on the southern side of the island, roughly where the two arms met. From there we had a clear view of the various buildings on the island. The manor was on the opposite shore, facing west. To the southwest of the manor were the island's other structures, one of which we assumed had once been Burgess's workshop, now converted, apparently, to house the clinic. We could also see a couple of cottages and a few other smaller buildings, the function of which weren't clear. There was also a large swimming pool, a gazebo, a couple of tiki huts, and even a raised area under the banyan trees from which we could hear the sound of a waterfall flowing. Beyond the pool, we could see what looked to be a large cage of some sort, but we couldn't see what might have been locked inside. On our side of the island we could see a man-made beach and a fishing dock, and further to the northeast of that, we saw a boathouse built adjacent to a covered slip dug into the soft rock of the island. Underneath the slip's roof was a heavy-duty lift from which hung an expensive, custom-built run-about. I guessed a channel led in there, because otherwise there wouldn't have been enough water on low tide for a heavy boat like that to have gotten in or out.

As we were giving the island a once-over, we could tell that a guard was also taking a look at us. However, the place where we fishing, probably a thousand feet to the southeast of the buildings, was heavily covered in scrub growing out of a jumble of limestone and what had once been coral. I'd guess we were at least hundred yards from where the guard was sitting in his cart. There was no way that he could get closer. We kept fishing.

"Kenny," I said. "It sure looks like they don't want anyone they don't invite to visit that island."

"You can say that again. I haven't seen security like that since I was building that telephone system down in Guyana. There were a bunch of drug lords and other guys who, for one reason or another, felt the need to have their own private armies. I learned quickly that when you went into a bar, you needed to be very careful about which girl you flirted with or who you picked a fight with. Those mercenary bastards didn't mess around. While I was there, they took out probably a half dozen guys who worked for me. We'd find them in the middle of the street, either with their throats cut or pumped full of lead. More often than not, their dicks would be cut off, too. But there was nothing we could ever do about it. All we could do was try to stay out of trouble."

"Shit!" I said. "That sounds bad. You think these guys would be like that?"

"It wouldn't surprise me. They've got the same look."

"So…you don't think there would be any way to get on that island?" I asked.

Kenny looked at me funny, then said, "I didn't say that. But why in the world would you want to do that? If those goons got hold of you, they would, without question, put a hurt on you."

"I just think that somebody ought to be taking a look to see if Tommy or his brother might be there," I said. "So how do you think somebody might be able to get on the island?"

"Jim, it wouldn't be easy. I'd bet that the place is covered with motion detectors that, if activated, would turn on all kinds of lights, alarms, bells, you name it. And, you told me that there are several heavily armed guards. Clearly, they don't want you there. I think you ought to give up on that idea."

"Kenny, I hear you. But you hinted a minute ago that you thought there might be a way to do it. Let's just talk hypothetically for a minute. If, for some reason, you wanted to get on that island to look around, how would you do it?"

"First, I'd need to find out if there are any gaps in the motion detectors that you could exploit. Without finding a gap, I'd give up on the idea. But, assuming there's some way to get on the island and not activate the alarms, I'd try to have someone create a distraction away from where I wanted to come onshore. Then I'd take a quick look around and get the hell out of there as quickly as I could. I would not want those guys to find me."

"I know. I know. But how could you take a look at the motion detectors?" I persisted. "Do you know about those kinds of things?"

"I don't really know that much about them," he replied. "I don't know how to disarm them or anything like that. But I used to install some of those systems, and from what I remember, they all use some kind of infrared light, which, if the beam is broken, causes an alarm to be activated. Back in the day, that used to be pretty high-tech. But now it's common, and you can go the Depot and get all kinds of motion-activated lights and alarms. But almost all of those cheaper homes use systems that emit a broad-based light distribution. The problem with them is you can't keep tree branches or other kinds of landscaping from triggering an alarm when they move in the wind. So that kind of system isn't used whenever security is really important. A system like what I'm sure they have on the island would use tightly focused infrared beams that run from a source to a specified receptor. The beams would be sited where there would be no interference from plants or limbs."

"So would there be just one beam?" I asked Kenny.

He laughed and said, "Oh, hell no. They'll have installed a whole web of those things, overlapping each other, and at all different heights. The whole point is to make it impossible for a person to come onto the island without them knowing it. And I'm sure that all the beams are linked back to a computer somewhere that will tell the guards exactly where there's been an intruder."

"How do the guards keep from setting them off?" I asked.

"The beams will be only sited along the perimeter of the property so that those inside can move without concern. And they'll have some way to deactivate the system whenever they want to let anyone in or out."

"OK, I've got all that. So how could you find out if there's any weakness or gap in the system? Hypothetically speaking, of course."

Kenny said, "Funny enough, it's not that hard to do. All you need is a night vision device."

"Yeah, right!" I responded. "Aren't those things all tightly controlled by the government to keep them out of the hands of terrorists?"

"No. Not anymore. The technology has evolved well beyond what it used to be. Now the military is onto generation four or five kind of stuff. Those latest iterations are government only—and expensive as hell. But the first-gen systems are now being sold to hunters. And you can get them for only a couple of hundred bucks at Bass Pro or any place like that."

"And a system like that would let you figure out if there's a gap in the alarm system?"

"Yeah, all you'd have to do, hypothetically speaking, would be to come out here on a dark night and take a look through the scope. The infrared beams would show up almost as bright as day. It'd be pretty simple, actually," he told me.

"Kenny, do you really know this? Or are you just assuming this?" I asked.

"Well, I know that's how we use to do it when we'd test the systems that we'd installed, just to make sure that we'd not left any gaps."

"So whoever installed the system here would probably have done the same thing?"

"Maybe. Maybe not. Not everyone who installs these things does as good as a job as I used to," he replied.

"Kenny, I don't think there's much of a moon this week," I commented.

"Yeah, I hear you. Did I mention that I saw in today's paper that Bass Pro has a big sale going on?"

Chapter Twenty-Six

When I got back to the house after cleaning the fish and dropping Kenny off, Jill told me that Juan Carlos had called and asked for me to call him back. I quickly did so.

"Juan Carlos, this is Jim Story. I wanted to get back to you as soon as I could. Were you able to find out anything about our Spanish doctor?"

"Jim, that's why I called. I knew you said it was important, so I wanted to get to you as soon as I could. Fortunately, when I called our credit area in Madrid, they knew exactly who I was asking about. Jim, I need to warn you that what I'm going to tell you is going to be hard to believe. It's almost like science fiction. I'll save you all the details and, how do you say it, just cut to the chase. The group that bought the island initially tried to borrow from our bank to fund it. Andalusia Properties has four owners. Dr. Areola owns fifty percent; the other half is owned equally by three very prominent Spaniards. According to my source, each of these men invested five million US dollars. Dr. Areola put up nothing. The group was looking to borrow an additional fifteen million, secured by the joint and several guarantees of the three investors. And trust me, they were all good for it. They are among the wealthiest men in the country. Ordinarily, this would have been a slam-dunk credit call. But...Dr. Areola's involvement was something we couldn't get comfortable with."

"Why is that? Did he default on his student loans or something?" I asked.

"No, Jim. It's more complicated than that," said Juan Carlos. "Let me tell you about him. First, Dr. Areola is a genius. He graduated at the top of his medical school class and then went into practice as a cardiac surgeon. He was one of the most respected in the country, probably in all of Europe. His specialty was heart transplants. But as time went by, he started to become frustrated by that process. Even in Spain, which has one of the highest organ donor rates in the world, there is always a shortage of organs available when they are needed. Consequently, he lost many patients whom he felt he would have otherwise been able to save if only organs had been available. But beyond that, he hated the complications that came from the body's rejection of transplanted tissue. In many cases, the rejections caused the transplants to fail entirely—or if they didn't fail, the chemicals needed to control rejection caused horrible side effects. It was almost too much for him to deal with. He hated failure. He couldn't stand that the state of medical knowledge was such that it couldn't deal with these failures. So he began, on the side, to research options for addressing this problem. Apparently, he'd learned about work being done in London to grow organs in the lab using the patient's own stem cells—the thought being that such organs would not be rejected since they were grown from the patient's own cells. As I understand it, the researchers in London were focused on using synthetic materials as the framework upon which the cells would grow. Apparently, they were using some miracle material they had developed called nanocomposite, which is resistant to infection and has pores the right size to hold the growing cells. But the researchers in London could only grow simple tissue structures, things like windpipes. They couldn't figure out how to get the cells to grow properly when they tried to replicate their success with more complex organs like the heart. And that's where Dr. Areola comes in. He discovered how to do it."

"I'd think the bank would want to bankroll something like that," I said.

"Ordinarily, you'd be right. But there's more to the story. What Areola discovered was that if you used the natural structure of the heart as the framework upon which to grow the cells, then the stem cells would somehow recognize that they needed to grow into the shape of a heart, or a lung, or a liver, or whatever you were trying to grow. It was truly a miraculous discovery. His initial work was done using rats. Of course, in that case, there was no difficulty in getting access to donor hearts, or whatever you needed. He'd take the heart from one individual, and then put it through a process using high-tech detergents to rinse away all the cells of the donor rat. What he'd be left with was an underlying scaffold of collagen that originally held the heart together. Then, stem cells taken from the recipient rat would be placed on the scaffolding, and all of this would be put into a bioreactor. The bioreactor would provide the right mix of nutrients, oxygen, and chemicals—much like a womb—to stimulate the growth of the heart cells. Over time this would produce a new heart for the patient, but one that his body wouldn't reject because it was made from his own cells."

"So," I said, "as you suggested earlier, let's cut to the chase. When it came to doing this for humans, where was he going to get the donor organs he needed to create the scaffolds to grow new organs?"

"Exactly. Now he was back to where he started, restricted by a shortage of donor organs. The bank could never get comfortable with how he planned to get around that obstacle."

"What do you mean?"

"He'd never give us a straight answer. Rather, as I understand it, he'd just blow the issue off, like it was something he wasn't really worried about. Eventually, we decided to decline the loan. But we heard that the group was able to get its funding from one of the 'cajas'—you know, one of the smaller community-based lending institutions in Spain."

"What about the guys who were putting the money into the group?" I asked. "Where'd they fit in?"

"That, too, was a little bit unusual," Juan Carlos replied. "They'd never invested together. We're not even sure if they knew each other. In fact, as far as we could tell, other than being extremely wealthy, they only had one thing in common."

I could tell that Juan Carlos was waiting for me to ask what that common element was. So, after the appropriate interval to allow the suspense to build, I did.

He replied, "They were all old—and all about to die from congestive heart failure."

"Shit!" I blurted. "Are you thinking what I'm thinking?"

Juan Carlos answered, "It has crossed my mind. I thought you ought to know as soon as possible."

"Thanks. I'll keep you posted."

Chapter Twenty-Seven

"Mike! This is Jim Story. Call me as soon as you can. I've figured out why there are so many people disappearing on the island. Call me!"

I'd called him on my cell, and left the message on his. I knew he'd get back as soon as he could. I sat down to wait. By seven, he still hadn't called, and I was starting to get hungry.

"Hey, babe. What're our plans for dinner?"

Jill replied, as I knew she would, "Why are you asking me? What is our plan?"

It was somewhat of a joke between Jill and me that everything had to be planned out. Hell, truthfully, it was a lot more than a joke. If there was one thing I was known for with our kids, it was the need to plan out just about every aspect of our lives. Spontaneity was not something I'd ever been big on.

"Just checking to make sure there's nothing in the oven," I said.

"I never got to Publix today. The cupboard's kind of bare," Jill replied.

"You want to go to Woody's?"

"Sounds like a plan. Give me a minute to change my clothes."

"I don't have to change, do I?"

Jill took a quick review of what I was wearing—exercise shorts and Columbia fishing shirt still stained with the evidence of the redfish expedition earlier in the day—and replied, "I don't want you to do anything that might jeopardize your reputation in town as being a crusty old fisherman, but if you expect me to sit at the same table as you, I'd suggest that you might want to get cleaned up before we go. When's the last time you had a shower?"

"Hey," I protested, laughing. "No reason to get testy. I had one yesterday."

"My point exactly. Now go in there and get cleaned up, and then we'll go get something to eat."

We walked into Woody's a little after seven thirty. I'd forgotten that it was open mike night. I knew we were in for some fun. All the bars and restaurants on the island were always trying to stage some kind of music to entice patrons to come in their doors. But during the summer, in the middle of the week, it was hard for any proprietor to justify the expense of actually paying a musician to perform. Thus, the genesis of open mike night—you can come sing as long as I don't have to pay you.

I didn't know the specifics of what Woody's had worked out with the guy charged with riding herd on the performers, but occasionally he'd play a song and then sidle up to the bar as the amateurs took their turns. I suspected that free drinks and tips may have been his compensation for the gig. His name was Rip—at least, that's what he went by on the island. He was actually an extremely talented musician and songwriter, but he seemed to really enjoy island life. I always suspected that some of that enjoyment may have led to that specific name becoming associated with him.

That night's talent was, to say the least, varied. There was one lady with a guitar who was actually pretty good, singing songs that we all knew and enjoyed. Then there was guy with a ukulele who needed a little more practice. Actually, he needed a lot more practice. Halfway through his performance his voice gave out. But that was probably a good thing. Rip got him a drink and suggested that he needed to go rest his voice. As the evening continued, four or five others took their turns, some good, some bad, but all fun. It helped to keep our minds off Little Bokeelia Island.

We were just finishing dinner when we noticed Steve and Katie Fairchild coming through the door. They were good friends of ours, and both had played key roles in helping to bring Carl Perez to justice. Steve was a big guy. He had played football at West Point—started there as a defensive back for three years. Once he graduated, he entered the army and led special forces units in some extremely unfriendly places. At least he did until he stepped on an IED in Afghanistan. After that, he spent over a year at Walter Reed, recovering from traumatic brain injuries and learning how to walk again. His injuries were such that he had to give up his military career, so he had retired and, with his wife Katie, moved to Saint James City. He was a hero to all of us, and we liked Katie, too.

We saw them looking for a table and waved them over to sit with us. We were glad to see them, and they appeared to be happy to see us as well. After all the hugs and handshakes, they sat down. I ordered a round of drinks, and we all started to catch up. Steve and Katie both love to fish, but Steve was always quick to let everyone know that Katie was the best fisherman in the family. I believed it. She seemed to be good at everything she did. She used to play golf for the Gators, and before that she water skied at Sea World. Now she was selling real estate, and I heard she was good at that, too.

Jill and Katie engaged in sharing kid/grandkid updates while Steve and I exchanged fish stories. He fished more than I did, and he was better at it. But for once, given the success that Kenny and I had enjoyed that morning, my fish tales could measure up to his. He was impressed.

There's always etiquette to be followed when fishermen talk about their successes. You can ask questions, but you can't ask too many. Usually, it's OK to inquire about what kind of bait was used. And asking how you rigged your tackle is a fair topic, too. But you're going to cross the line if you try to find out exactly where the fish was caught. Some information is usually not meant to be inquired about, even among friends.

But that night I couldn't contain myself. I was so excited about that thirty-one inch bull red that I just went ahead and told Steve that we had been fishing just south of Little Bokeelia Island.

As I mentioned that, I noticed the happy twinkle in Steve's eyes fade, slowly replaced by a more serious look. "Any sign of Tommy?" he asked.

"No. Nothing."

"If you don't mind me asking, how come y'all were fishing so far north? That's a long way to run."

I thought about kidding Steve with my usual excuses for why we had gone up there, but I knew from the look in his eyes that it would have been a waste of time. "I guess I just wanted to get a better look at that island," I said.

"What'd you see?" he asked.

"Well, the guards are still there—and still as attentive as ever. We saw a helicopter come and go. And we kind of scoped out the eastern side of the island."

"Why'd you do that?" Steve asked perceptively.

"I guess I was just trying to find out if there was a way to get on the island so I could take a look around," I told him.

"And?" he probed.

"Kenny and I talked about it a lot. His guess is that the place is wired with motion detectors, and it would be hard to do. But if we could find a gap in the sensors, it might not be impossible. We'd need to create a distraction to amuse the guards. With that, I might be able to get through."

Steve answered, "I'm good at creating distractions."

"Hopefully, it won't come to that," I said. "I've got some information that I want to give Mike Collins that might get him off his ass to go take a look at that place." I took a quick look at my cell and added, "I've been waiting for him to return my call."

With that, Katie said, "If you're waiting for a call in here, you'll be waiting a long time. The tin roof over the building blocks out all the signals. You'll need to go outside if you want any reception."

"Shit!" I exclaimed. "I'd forgotten all about that. Y'all excuse me a minute while I walk outside to see if he's called."

When I returned, in response to their questioning looks, I shook my head no.

Jill said, "I told them about what Juan Carlos told you."

I looked at them and rolled my eyes. "Isn't that the strangest thing you've ever heard? It's like something right out of a damned science fiction movie, with a mad scientist growing human organs on a secret island. I'll be surprised if Mike Collins doesn't have me locked up in the loony ward when he hears about this."

"Well," Steve said. "If he doesn't take you seriously, you let me know. It sure sounds like someone needs to look into what's going on out there. If he won't do it, then I'd bet that you, Kenny, and I could pull it off."

We all just stared at each other, probably each reflecting back on the last time we all decided to take the law into our own hands, and how close that had gotten us to being killed.

Chapter Twenty-Eight

Jill and I tried to sleep in, probably because we had been slightly over served at Woody's. For some reason that seemed to happen regularly whenever we go there. But on this particular morning, we only succeeded in staying in bed five minutes longer than normal, because the dog, I assume, was not in the same condition as we were. Instead, she was pacing as energetically and insistently as ever, trying to make sure that we knew it was already past the time for her breakfast and walk. So, reluctantly, we stumbled downstairs to take care of those chores, grumbling as we did. Twenty minutes later, when those were done, we settled down to drink some desperately needed coffee and tea. We had just gotten into our second cups when the phone rang. I could see that it was Mike Collins.

"Collins," I grumbled. "Why can't you call at a more reasonable hour?"

"What's the matter, big guy? Did you have too much fun last night?"

I could tell from the sound of his voice that he was feeling especially chipper. Just what I needed—a happy cop.

"Yeah. I guess we must have. It's kind of hard to remember all the details. But that's probably not something you should tell the fuzz, is it?"

"Hey! I'm not in the traffic division any longer. My lips are sealed."

"Sure they are. You going to be out this way later? Maybe around noon?"

"Can be. If I have a good reason. You got something?"

"Yeah," I said. "I think so. How about the Waterfront?"

"I'll be there."

We chose an outside table, at the south end of the deck, as far away from several tables of hungry, happily chatting vacationers as could get. While we were waiting for our unsweetened teas to arrive, I asked him how the follow-up on the drug bust on the island had turned out.

"That turned out good," he answered. "I'm pretty sure that they won't be peddling pills out of there, or anywhere else, for some time to come. We've still got a bunch of deputies tracking down all the Capers who had been using the place. There's probably not much we can do to them, but it sure is a lot of fun to see the looks on their faces when we come to their doors."

"I could tell," I said, "that you were in a great mood, for some reason. Guess that explains it."

"Yeah. I really get off on scaring old people. Story, in case you can't tell, I'm being sarcastic. You need to give me more credit than that."

"Sorry. Were you able to tie any of the disappearances on the island to that operation?" I asked.

"No, we weren't. Just the rumor about the one girl who'd gotten greedy. Nothing else."

"I didn't think that you would," I said. "But I've got some information from Spain that I hope might get your attention."

"That's good. We didn't get anything from Interpol that was of any use. Just basic background stuff, but nothing to get us stirred up. What have you got?"

"Have you ever heard of organ farming?"

"Oh, shit! I knew that, coming from you, it was going to be something weird. I assume you're talking about human organs? If so, I've heard about buying organs from China, and I've heard about killing people for their organs down in South America. But I've never heard about growing them on a fucking farm. Are you trying to tell me that the 'Mango Factory' is branching out into another line of business?"

"Mike," I said. "Hear me out. This is serious. It's not bullshit. You need to pay attention to what I'm going to tell you."

"OK. Don't get sensitive on me. The sheriff's bad enough. What've you got?"

It took ten minutes telling him what I'd learned from Juan Carlos. I could tell that Mike was trying to take it all in, but at the same time, I could tell that he was having a hard time buying it.

When I had finished, he said, "So, bottom line, what you're suggesting is that this Spanish dude, on a little island off the tip of Bokeelia, is chopping people up so he can use their parts to grow organs to transplant into wealthy sick guys?"

"Exactly!" I answered.

Collins responded, "Jesus Christ! I should have known better than to drive out here to have lunch with you. Story. This is Pine Island, for God's sake. It's in the middle of nowhere. It's desolate. It's wet. There're mosquitoes out here. The biggest business on the whole damn island is picking crabs—at least it is now that we've closed down the pill mill. There aren't that many people out here who have college degrees. Hell, there ain't that many out here who can even read. Growing organs, like you're suggesting, is something high-tech. Really high-tech. This kind of stuff would have to be done somewhere like John's Hopkins, or the Mayo Clinic, or someplace like that. Not on fucking Pine Island!"

"Why not? Maybe this is the perfect place. It's quiet. It's out of the way. There's good air transportation in and out of the area. You can't get onto Little Bokeelia unless you're invited. It's easily guarded. There're enough buildings there to house the kind of operation we're talking about. And we know that Dr. Areola bought the place, or at least a group that he's a part of did. I can't see them buying it just to go fishing, can you?"

"No," Mike answered. "That wouldn't make any sense. But it doesn't mean that they're killing people out there to grow organs, either. Maybe it's just a nice quiet place for wealthy patients to come recover after having a transplant in Spain."

"Could be," I replied. "But I think you need to go out there and take a look around and try to find out what's really going on."

"Contrary to our reputation, we don't usually make a habit of harassing people."

"Can't you just make a social call? You know, just to offer your services, or something? Hell, this guy is a lot more suspicious-looking than the rest of us on the island, and that doesn't seem to stop your department from keeping a close watch on us."

"Don't sell yourself short," Mike replied.

"Mike, you need to get out there and look around. And don't forget that Tommy may still be alive. I don't think there's any time to waste."

"Tommy got drunk, and fell out of his fucking boat."

"No, he didn't. I know that, and you know that. So are you going to go out there, or do I need to do that?"

"Yeah, I'll get some guys together, and we'll get out there this afternoon. I'll have to admit that you've gotten my curiosity up. And Story, I'd stay away from there, if I were you."

"Let me know what you find," I said.

"I'll give you a call tonight."

Chapter Twenty-Nine

Seven o'clock. Jill and I were ready to tune in to what we knew would be another night of stimulating television (not!). We always start with a rousing edition of *Wheel of Fortune*. I was never very good at the show, but Jill was. Actually, I used the first spin of the wheel as my signal that it was time to pour the first of my evening's scotch and waters. I had just put the ice in my glass when the phone rang. Mike Collins calling. I beat Jill to the phone.

"Mike," I said, perhaps a little too eagerly, and certainly not beating around the bush, "did you get out to Little Bokeelia today?"

"Yeah, we did. And we had a look around. Jim, I've got to tell you, I think you're barking up the wrong tree this time."

"What'd you find?"

"We pulled up to the front dock, two boats, three of us in each Zodiac," he told me. "We went in anticipating trouble, but we couldn't have been any more wrong. As soon as they recognized who we were, the guards put their guns away and helped tie us off to the dock. The head guy was a well-built, mean-looking German dude by the name of Kottmeyer. I figured him to probably be an uptight, unfriendly type. But I was wrong. As soon as I stepped on the dock, he shook my hand and asked how he could be of help. None of the others seemed suspicious or jumpy, not in the least. I introduced myself, and told him that I'd like to meet with Dr. Areola. He walked down the dock, maybe twenty feet away from me, and got on his radio. I could tell he was speaking Spanish. A few minutes later he came back. He apologized and explained that the doctor was currently tied up in the laboratory, but that he would be able to meet with me in about an hour. I told him that would be fine, and asked if it would be possible for us to look around the island while we waited. He again got on the radio but quickly came back to say that he would be happy to show us around. One of my sergeants came with me, and we climbed onboard Kottmeyer's golf cart. He drove us to the south tip of the island, and then we worked our way back up, taking a good look at everything. We saw the cottages, although we didn't go in. Kottmeyer explained that some of his men were asleep in one after pulling their shift the previous night. The door on the other was locked on the outside with a padlock. He dismissed that cottage, saying that currently it was only used as a storeroom. We continued to look around. But nothing looked unusual or out of place. We didn't, however, go into the lab. Kottmeyer said that Dr. Areola would show that to us later, explaining that since the Doctor was so proud of it, he liked to personally do that tour. After that we took a good look around the pool, saw the waterfall and all the trees that Edison planted."

"Did you see the cage?" I asked.

"Yes, we did," he replied. "I'll tell you more about that in a minute."

"Did he offer you a 'mai-tai'?" I asked.

"As a matter of fact, he did. Why do you ask?

"Because it sounds to me like he was leading you around just like a damned time-share salesman, making sure you saw what they wanted you to see and nothing else."

"Maybe. But it wasn't like I had any choice. Remember, I didn't have a warrant, and I damned sure wasn't going to be able to get one."

"So did you ever get to see the doctor?" I asked.

"Yeah. Kottmeyer took us to the main house and asked us to wait in the library. We were there about twenty minutes before the doctor came in and introduced himself. He's a mid-forty-ish-looking guy, with an olive skinned complexion. I figured it to be just what you might expect from a full-blood Spaniard. However, I got the clear impression that he doesn't spend much time in the sun. I couldn't see any sign of a sunburn, tan line, or freckles. And there were certainly no raccoon eyes—you know, like all of us down here have from wearing sun glasses. I'd bet he spends a lot of time in the lab. In terms of stature, I'd guess that he's probably a little less than six feet tall and weighs maybe one eighty. He looked to me like he was in good shape, but not really like he spends a lot of time in the gym. I'd wager that he's kind of hyperactive—you know, the kind of guy who's too busy to sit still long enough for a calorie to have any chance to turn to fat. Bottom line, I guess he looks just like you would expect any young doctor to look. Slender, good health, and a little bookish. He was wearing scrubs. Our conversation went as follows:

"'Lieutenant Collins, I notice your badge and weapon. Are you are with local law enforcement?'

"'Yes,' I said. 'I am the lead investigator for the Gulf Islands Division of the Lee County Sheriff's Office.'

"I didn't embellish, waiting for his reaction. But he didn't miss a beat, getting right to the point. "'Lieutenant Collins, why are you here?'

"I said, 'Dr. Areola, there are a couple of reasons. First, it's come to my attention that no one from the Sheriff's office has come to welcome you to Lee County. That's an oversight on our part. We always want to do that and to get to know any new business owners in the area. We want you to know that you can call on us if you ever need our help. Second, I have to admit that there are many questions, and rumors, on the island about you, and what you are doing out here. Truthfully, I have the same questions. And you know it's funny, in my line of work, I can't stand unanswered questions. So, I thought that while I was here I'd ask you those questions personally.'

"He said, 'Lieutenant Collins, thank you for your visit. Should we ever need your services we will certainly call you. But let me correct one thing you just said. We are not a business. The only activities on this island are my personal research projects. I am familiar with your laws. I understand that if I was engaged in business here, I would need to be registered with your county and pay business taxes. But I assure you, that is not the case. I am engaged only in private research. In many ways, what I am doing is similar to what Dr. Burgess did when he owned this island— and similar to what Mr. Edison did in his backyard when he lived in Fort Myers.'

"'I hope you will be as successful as those two,' I said. 'What kind of research are you conducting?'

"He just said, 'Medical research,' kind of curtly.

"I asked him, 'Dr. Areola, my sources tell me that you may be involved in human organ farming. Would that be the type of medical research in which you are engaged?'

"He laughed quietly, shook his head, and smiled. Then he said, 'Lieutenant, organ farming is such an ugly term. I can assure you that I am not a farmer. I do not grow crops to be harvested and sold at the public market. I am a doctor and a researcher, engaged in the study of how to prevent needless human death. Granted, farmers may come later to tend the fields planted with seeds that I develop. But no, I am not a farmer. However, your sources are correct to suggest that human organs are the focus of my research. As you may know, for several years I was an acclaimed heart surgeon in Europe, performing hundreds of transplants each year. But despite all of my success, despite all of my fame, and despite the wealth that came with that, I was tormented. Tormented because the success rate of the transplants I performed, the highest rate in the world, was still much too low. Tormented because, even when the transplants were successful, the patients' quality of life was not always good. And I was tormented by the number of patients who died while waiting to be matched with a suitable donor heart. In my mind, what I was doing, what I had been trained to do, was not really good medicine. I felt like I was nothing more than a very highly paid plumber. What I was doing was, perhaps, better than doing nothing, but it was not good medicine. I could possibly help a relatively small number of patients, but I could not really cure them. And, unfortunately, nothing could be done to help the millions of others living with terminal heart disease. There had to be a better way. And that is why I am here.'

"'Dr. Areola, your story is interesting,' I told him. 'Without question, heart disease is terrible. I know that personally. My father died from congestive heart failure, and during the years before his death, his quality of life was terrible. And I know that, with my genes, I can likely look forward to the same outcome. It sounds to me like you are doing wonderful work. But I have to ask, why are you doing that work here? Why not in Madrid? Why not in Barcelona?'

"He said, 'Lieutenant, it is perhaps hard for you to understand, but in the world of medical research it is sometimes better to labor out of the public view. Over the years I have learned that the medical community, unfortunately, is an extremely jealous one. It does not like when its accepted methodologies are challenged. A huge industry, all around the world, has been built over the past decades to support the existing manner in which heart transplants are performed. Today, whatever country you are in, the largest donations go to support this industry, the most modern buildings on medical campuses are devoted to cardiac care, and the brightest surgeons make extravagant incomes by working in this area. No one, and I mean no one, wants to see this orthodoxy challenged. Over time I came to understand this. That is why I am now so sensitive to security on this island. I learned that if I questioned the status quo, I would eventually be shunned and ridiculed, and I would lose my privileges to operate at the best hospitals. So that is why it is better that I do my research here, in obscurity, hidden off the coast of Pine Island. I still perform transplants in Europe, but now I only devote half of my time to that pursuit. Honestly, now I prefer to spend as much time as possible here, working on my research.'

"I asked, 'Has your research been successful?'

"When I asked this question, I noticed the doctor's eyes light up and saw the furrows on his brow disappear. In fact, his whole countenance seemed to change. His expression went from one of frustration and impatience to a look that I can only describe as one of being at peace. He said, 'Lieutenant, please come with me, and I will show you the results.'

"I followed, leaving my sergeant with Kottmeyer. He led me out a side door of the manor. We followed a stone path under the banyans and stood in front of the large steel cage next to the pool. He asked me, 'Lieutenant Collins, what do you see in the cage?'

"I said, 'It looks to me like a gorilla—a very large gorilla. I'd guess it is a mature male, a silverback.'

"He said, 'You have answered as most people would. And, yes your sexual identification is correct. But I do not describe this magnificent animal as a gorilla. Instead, I prefer to describe this splendid creature as being the savior of mankind.'

"'What do you mean?' I asked. 'If you start to tell me that you're planning to establish a new religion out here, I'm going to go ahead and arrest you on the spot. Lee County's already had too much of that crap in its past.'

"He said, 'No, I am not a religious person. Rather, I am a man of science. I understand that the gorilla is the animal species that genetically and functionally is the most similar to humans. We differ from that animal in only minor, relatively unimportant ways. The similarity between the great ape and man is very important to my research. Now, please, follow me.'

"We retraced our path toward the manor, but when the stone path branched to the right, we followed that. That path split a little further along, and we took the one that went to the left. It led to the north door of the building that had once been Dr. Burgess's workshop. I followed Dr. Areola inside. When he turned on the lights, I was amazed at what I was seeing. There were several large glass containers, each attached to a maze of wires and hoses, and each glowing and bubbling like those old fashioned Christmas lights you used to see. And inside each glass tube was what looked to me like a living, beating heart. One was large; a couple were smaller.

"'Lieutenant,' he said, 'what do you see now?'

"'Dr. Areola, I may not know what I'm looking at, but it sure looks to me like you are growing human hearts in here.'

"He said, 'You are close. But from a technical standpoint, I will argue that the hearts are actually growing themselves. I am not growing them. I have merely provided the conditions that are necessary for them to grow. The glass containers that you are seeing are called bioreactors, but I prefer to think of them as being like the wombs of our mothers, where we all grew from a single fertilized cell into the complex creatures that we were at birth. We often talk about the miracle of birth, but the real miracle is what takes place in the womb. That single stem cell develops, over the course of nine months, into a perfectly formed, intricate, and complex human body. And now, I have learned to duplicate a part of that process. I have learned how to allow a patient's own stem cells to develop into a perfectly formed human heart that can be used to replace his own diseased heart, without risk of rejection, without risk of side effects. To me, it is truly miraculous. With this technique I can finally truly cure my patients. Now, when they leave the surgery, they will once again be healthy, with their own hearts beating as strongly as they did when they were young.'

"I said, 'Doctor, I am stunned. If what you are saying is true, this will be the greatest advance in medicine that the world has ever seen.'

"He said, 'No, I will disagree strongly with that statement. This is merely another step, a relatively small step, along the path of medical progress. Is this a greater advance than when doctors in the Middle Ages first diagrammed the skeletal system? Is this a greater advance than when the importance of using antiseptics was discovered? Is this more important than the development of antibiotics? No. This is just another small step along the path. But it is a step that will make me feel much better about what I have chosen to do with my life.'

"I said, 'I can appreciate that sentiment. Men of good intent want, at the end of the day, to feel that their lives have made a positive difference. When I arrest a criminal, it makes me feel that I have done something good. I know it pales in comparison to what you are doing, but at least it's something. Dr. Areola, there is one thing, though, that I don't understand about what you have told me. How does the single stem cell that you put in the bioreactor know to grow into a heart and not an eyeball or a big toe?'

"He said, 'Lieutenant, you are very intelligent. That, in fact, was the key obstacle that needed to be overcome to make this process work. And at the end of the day, the answer proved to be remarkably simple. What we have learned is that if a stem cell is placed to grow on the underlying structure of an organ, the cartilage that holds the organ together, then the cell somehow knows that based on the structure upon which it is placed, it should rep-licate that particular organ. To grow a heart, for example, all that is needed is the clean supporting cartilage from an actual heart. To get that cartilage we subject a donor heart to a strong bath of detergent-like chemicals and slowly clean away everything but the underlying cartilage. Then, when a stem cell is placed on that structure, somehow it knows to develop into a heart. The doc-tors in Europe have been trying, without success, to use synthetic structures as the frameworks upon which to grow organs. I have learned that it is much better, in fact it is imperative, that you must use a naturally occurring, and naturally similar, structure if you are to successfully grow replacement organs. Experiments have shown that the ideal structure would come from using the carti-laginous structure from another human heart. But that, of course, presents challenges. The patient, obviously, can't let us use his own heart for several months while we grow him a new one. And, as I have explained previously, the supply of human donor hearts is very limited, since the demand for transplants is so high. I have tried for years to get in line for a portion of that supply stream, but unfortunately, I have been met with nothing but hostility. The limited hearts available from donors is simply too valuable to the heart transplant industry to allow them to be used for experimen-tation. So I have had to turn to alternatives. Now, do you remem-ber the gorilla that we saw earlier?'

"I said, 'Don't tell me that you are going to kill that monkey out there so you can use the cartilage in its heart.'

"'No. Not that gorilla. He is my pet. I keep him there to remind me of how beautiful, and how precious, gorillas' lives are. It's impor-tant, I think, to never lose sight of that. But I have learned that the cartilage from a gorilla's heart is genetically the same as that from a human heart. A human stem cell, if placed upon that structure and properly nourished in a bioreactor, will develop into a perfectly formed human heart that can be transplanted without risk of rejection. The hearts that you see in this room have all been grown using underlying structures from gorillas. And they are all perfect.'

"I said, 'Surely, Dr. Areola, there must be a smaller supply of gorilla hearts available to you than human hearts? After all, the gorilla is almost extinct in the wild.'

"He said, 'What you say is true. Today, the supply of hearts from gorillas is extremely limited. But I have established relationships with the largest zoos in the world. I have been blessed to have a number of very wealthy investors in my work. And at my request, they have each made sizeable donations to these zoos. In exchange, the zoos now send me the hearts of any of their gorillas that die. And that is what I use for these experiments—and what I have used as the basis for several hearts that I have recently successfully transplanted into patients in Spain. The technique works. All that is needed now is an expanded supply of gorilla hearts. And I believe that there is no reason, given the proper financial incentives, that gorillas cannot be raised on a sufficiently large scale to supply enough heart cartilage to meet the foreseeable demand for heart transplants in the entire Western world.'

"After that explanation, I was at a loss of anything else to say, or to ask. I felt that I was clearly in the presence of a genius—a man who could, and would, change the world. It was almost as if I were standing there talking with Thomas Edison. For the first time in my life, I was absolutely at a loss for words.

"Dr. Areola, sensing my predicament, escorted me out of the lab and walked toward the dock where I could see Kottmeyer, my sergeant, and the other deputies waiting. As we walked, the doctor thanked me for coming. I thanked him for showing me what he had developed. As we neared the boats, he quietly asked that I not share what I had seen any further than what was required by policy. He explained that the financial implications of this news leaking out prematurely could be devastating to his investors. I assured him that this information would only go into my report, and only to those with a need to know. I thanked him for his hospitality, and we left."

"So, Mike, I have a need to know?" I asked.

"Fuck, Story, you're the reason we went out there in the first place. As far as I can tell, right now you're the only one that has a need to know."

"Mike, I've only got one question."

"What's that?" he asked.

"Would you know the difference between heart cartilage from a gorilla and that from a human?"

"Damn, Story, you're the most suspicious guy I've ever met. You must have been a banker too long."

"Probably," I replied. "But knowing how to sniff out bullshit is the first thing you're taught in banker's school. I thought detectives had to take that course, too."

"Just when I was starting to feel good about the future of the human race, and what do you do? You just pissed all over my fucking good mood," Mike grouched. "I guess I'll just go back to harassing old farts. Thanks for reminding me that, in my line of work, I can't trust a single living soul. That's more than a little bit depressing. Jim, I don't know what to tell you. I didn't see anything out there to make me suspicious in the least. It all looked to be on the up and up."

"Mike, let me ask you one more question. When you went into the workshop building, did the doctor's lab occupy the whole building?"

"No. As a matter of fact, it didn't. I'd guess it took up maybe a third of the total building. I did notice that there was a door that led out of the lab into what I would presume to be the rest of the building. I asked the doctor where the door led. He told me that there was nothing there currently, just the remains of Dr. Burgess's old workshop. He said that he would build it out if he ever needed more space."

"Did you believe him?" I asked.

"I had no reason not to," he said. "Truthfully, Jim, after meeting Dr. Areola, after witnessing his passion for his work and his enthusiasm for helping mankind, I think I would believe anything that man ever told me. I was impressed."

"I can tell. Mike, I appreciate you going out there to take a look, and I very much appreciate you telling me what you found. I have to admit that it looks like I might be wrong about this one."

"Jim, I think you are. Let's stay in touch."

Chapter Thirty

The next day, a little after noon, I gave Kenny a call. "Kenny, guess what UPS just delivered?" I said when he picked up.

"Did you finally buy that stuff on TV that guarantees to make you longer, stronger, and irresistible to women of all ages?" he asked.

"Cute. You know I don't need any of that stuff," I told him. "But I got something that's even more exciting. I'm opening, as we speak, a box from Bass Pro that contains a night vision monocular guaranteed to let one see clearly in the darkest night."

"Whooeee! That's exciting. There's no telling what kind of trouble we could get into with that thing. It would be a lot of fun to use it to scope out the dark corners behind Froggy's on a Friday night. There's no telling who we might see, and what they might be doing. But Jim, really, did you buy it for what I think you bought it for?"

"I thought it might be useful for night fishing."

"Night fishing! What do you mean?" he asked innocently.

"You know, Kenny, like when we go fishing at night and need to see if there are any gaps in a motion detection system," I said.

"Perfect. And you know, there's not much moon tonight. It might be a good night to go fishing."

"That's why I'm calling. I'll pick you up at nine o'clock."

"You're asking a lot, you know," he told me.

"What do you mean?" I asked.

"I'm usually drunk and in bed by then."

"I hear you. Me, too. Maybe, we need to take a nap this afternoon, and be careful about what we drink."

"I've got you. You want me to bring any shrimp?" he asked.

"Sounds good," I replied. "Who knows, we might actually need to see what's biting after the sun goes down. And you probably ought to bring a little beer, too. You know, just to make it all look right if anyone gets curious."

"Nine o'clock."

Chapter Thirty-One

I liked to take the boat out at night. Jill didn't. In fact, she flatly refused to go with me. Then again, she had more than enough doubts about my boating skills, even in the middle of the day. But the dark didn't worry me. I guess that's because of how I grew up. When I was a kid, I spent a lot of time on boats, and a fair amount of that time was spent knocking around in the dark. One of my fondest childhood memories is of poking around in the dark in a small flat-bottomed boat among the mangroves that line the edge of Tampa Bay. I spent a lot of time doing that with my dad, cast netting mullet. Doing that was a lot of fun for a kid, and I learned in a hurry to not be scared of boating in the dark. Another thing I learned was about how good freshly caught mullet can taste when they're fried up around midnight, immediately after a long night of throwing a heavy net. Fried mullet, grits, hush puppies, and baked beans! Even now my mouth starts watering just thinking about it.

But that night I didn't think we'd be doing any cooking. Still, just in case we got hungry, I packed some sandwiches, and several cans of Vienna sausage. No way that we were going to starve.

I gave Jill a kiss good-bye and told her to expect us back by midnight. I also told her if we weren't back by then, and if she hadn't heard from me on my cell, then she should call Mike Collins and tell him were we had been.

I idled down the canal to Kenny's house. He was standing on the seawall when I got there. Actually, he was standing on the seawall, fishing, throwing a top-water Mirrorlure, hoping to fool a hungry snook into ambushing the plug.

"Any luck?" I asked.

"Actually, yeah," he replied. "I landed two small ones and one that was pretty good-sized. I'll be glad when they reopen the season for these things. I'm about ready for a snook sandwich."

I laughed. "That sounds good. I hear they're going to lift the ban this fall."

Kenny agreed. "That's what I hear, too. It makes sense to me. There are a lot of them around now."

"All right, Kenny, let me give you a hand with your stuff." I took his rod and placed it in the rod rack behind the leaning post. He then handed me the bait bucket, which he'd loaded with a couple dozen hand-picked shrimp. Redfish love them. Then I took hold of his fabric cooler as he handed it down to me.

"Damn, Kenny, how much beer'd you put in this thing?" I asked.

"Oh, Jim, there's only a couple of six packs. You know, just enough for me. I know you don't like that stuff."

"I gotcha," I replied. "But you better go easy on that stuff until we've had a chance to look around up there. We don't want to look suspicious."

"Hell, Jim," Kenny replied. "The way I figure it, it'd look real suspicious to anyone that knows me if I wasn't half crocked. Don't worry. I'll be all right."

We pushed away from the dock and headed down the canal. As we left civilization, and headed into the mangroves, Kenny asked, "Did you bring the scope?"

"Yeah. You want to take a look?"

"If I could," Kenny replied. "Is it ready to go?"

"I think so. Here, take a look, and let me know what you think."

I handed the night vision device to him. He turned it on, put it up to his eye, and looked into the dark toward where we were headed.

"Does it work?" I asked.

"Damn, Jim, this thing is good," Kenny replied. "It's a lot better than what I used to use. This'll work fine. If there are any gaps in the security system, we should be able to pick them up pretty easily."

A few minutes later, we were headed up the sound. It was truly a dark night. Not only was there no moon, but there was a cloud cover that prevented any starlight from helping us see. Fortunately, the wind was still, and there was no chop on the water. With no light, and with little noise from the four-stroke outboard, it almost seemed like we were floating through the air. It was a cool sensation. One of the reasons I liked going out at

THE CUT BAIT MURDERS

night was that, with the normal things I sensed blacked out, my mind had to focus differently. I felt like that was a healthy thing; I liked it.

In the dark, boats that were underway were required to display a certain pattern of lights. For a boat at anchor, a different light was required. Therefore, it really was not difficult to deal with other boats on the sound (as long as they were obeying the rules and displaying the proper lights). Some things you just had to take on faith. I had dimmed the lighting of the GPS unit's display so that looking at it wouldn't destroy my night vision. With that setting, it was easy to keep track of where we were on the sound. I wasn't worried at all about running up on an oyster bar or anything like that. Truthfully, the only thing about running a boat at night that worried me was the possibility of running into something like an unlit channel marker. When I was a kid, I had a friend who had done just that. Fortunately for my friend, his sturdy Stump Knocker skiff had just glanced off the pole, and he had been all right. But that event made a big impression on me back then, and I worried about it every time I was out at night. To minimize that risk, this particular night I just followed the well-traveled path on my GPS. Unless there was just something floating around out there, I figured we should be all right.

Another thing I liked about boating at night was that you don't have to deal with much traffic. Although there may be a few commercial guys knocking about, there normally are absolutely no recreational boaters to worry about. It was almost like having the sound to yourself.

Thirty-eight minutes after taking off, we angled away from the main channel and headed up the cut that ran behind Useppa

Island. From there we slid through the gap between Patricio and Broken Islands and on toward Little Bokeelia. I took pains to stay well away from the front side of the island; we quickly turned toward the south, where, after about a half mile, I picked up the narrow, unmarked channel that ran along the backside of the island. Although it was unmarked, I knew it had good water. I've seen the commercial guys out of Bokeelia travel it in some pretty big boats. As soon as we neared the mangroves on the south shore, we put down the Talon shallow-water anchor and broke out the fishing rods. We were using shrimp suspended under popping corks to keep the bait off the bottom. It took just a few minutes for the action to start. At almost the same time, both of our corks disappeared under the water, each heading quickly toward the sanctuary of the mangrove roots. We both set our hooks. Kenny connected, but I apparently pulled the hook out of the fish's mouth.

"Holy shit!" Kenny yelled, having totally forgotten about the need to maintain any degree of tactical obscurity. "Jim, this is a big fish," he grunted as he leaned against the pull on the line. I couldn't make out the fish in the dark, but I could see the commotion it was creating in the water due to the phosphorescence exploding in the dark.

"Is it a red, or a snook?" I asked.

"The way it's pulling, I'm pretty sure it's a big red," Kenny whispered. "I just hope I can keep him out of the roots."

I could hear Kenny starting to wheeze. He had a mild case of COPD, and sometimes, when he got excited, it flared up, making it hard for him to breathe.

"You all right, big guy?" I asked.

"Yeah. I'm fine," Kenny gasped. "I think I've finally got him [deep breath], I've finally got him headed my way. Get the [deep breath] landing net ready."

"Got it. Bring him in."

A couple of minutes later, the fish was alongside the boat, and Kenny led him in front of the landing net, just like you're supposed to. A second later the fish was in the boat. At that point, any pretense of silence went out the door. It was a big fish, and it was doing its dead level best to let us know that it was not happy about being out of the water. A redfish has a big, broad, strong tail, and it was beating it against the deck of the *Pulapanga* with all its might. It was making a hell of a racket. As was Kenny—he was excited.

"Whooeee! Do you see the size of that thing?" Kenny asked, loudly enough so that the folks sleeping all the way over in Bokeelia could certainly have heard the question.

"Damn right," I replied. "That is a big fish. One of the biggest ones we've ever put in this boat. But that could be a problem, you know?"

"Jim, what do you mean?" Kenny asked.

"We've got to measure this thing. I think it's too big!"

"What do you mean, too big? It's over the minimum size, and I'm pretty sure it'll fit in the live well."

"Come on, Kenny. You know as well as I do that there's a slot limit on these things. They've got to be at least eighteen inches long, but they can't be any more than twenty-seven inches long. We've got to measure this guy. I bet he's well over thirty inches."

I laid him down on the fish rules ruler. I was right; the fish was almost thirty-four inches long.

CHAPTER THIRTY-ONE

"Kenny, he's got to go back," I told him. "He's way too big."

"Shit," Kenny gasped. "I know. I know. But that always makes me mad, to have to put a fish like that back in. I could make one hell of a pot of redfish chowder with a fish like that. But you're right. Put him back."

I slid the fish into the water, and in no time, it had regained its composure, flicked that broad tail, and disappeared into the dark water.

"All right, Captain," Kenny said. "Now what?"

"Why don't I keep fishing for a while? But I think you need to take a little break. Maybe you can sit up there on that fishing chair, swivel it over toward Little Bokeelia, drink some beer, and see what you can see."

So that's what we did for the next hour. We used the trolling motor to ease us gradually along the mangroves while, just coincidentally, working our way along the parallel coast of Little Bokeelia Island. I caught a couple of small snook and several mangrove snappers, but no more redfish. While I was fishing, Kenny didn't say too much, but I could tell he was enjoying his beer. Periodically, he'd put the scope down and move us along with the trolling motor. Then, as soon as we'd anchored again, up would go the scope, and he'd go back to analyzing the infrared beams on the far shore, savoring his Bud Light as he did. Finally, just as I ran out of shrimp, Kenny spoke up. "OK, I think I've found it. Jim, why don't you take a look through this thing?"

He handed me the scope.

"Where should I look?" I asked.

"You see the outline of the main house? Take a look at the water line, just to the right of that. Tell me what you see."

"Damn," I exclaimed. "Look at all those green lines. They really stand out. Are those the infrared beams of the system?"

"Yep," Kenny answered. "You see the gap?"

"No. I can't say that I do. What am I supposed to be looking at?"

"Jim, can you see the dock that leads to the boathouse? Now, take a close look at where the dock and the boathouse meet. Then tell me what you see."

"OK. OK." I focused on that spot, trying to see what Kenny had discovered. It took me a couple of minutes, but finally I found what he wanted me to see. "Kenny, I think I see the gap. It looks like one beam ends on the outside of the left side of the dock, while the beam on the right ends on the outside of the support on that side. Is that what you're talking about?"

"Exactly!" he replied. "Each beam has a projector and, on the other end, a receptor. You can see that in this case, the receptors are mounted on the outsides of the support posts that hold up the roof over the boat slip, leaving a clear gap in between. They probably did that on purpose so that the boat can come and go without setting off the alarm. Or maybe, they just did it by mistake. Regardless, there is a clear path onto the island where you won't set off the motion sensors. Just swim up to the ladder at the end of the dock, climb up, and I think you can walk right in. You want to try it now?"

"Kenny, you better lay off that beer. There's no way I'm going onto that island until we've got a plan to distract those Nazis guarding the place. I've seen them up close, and they are serious about their jobs."

"Yeah. I hear you. But before we leave, why don't you take a look around the rest of the island with that scope and tell me what else you see?"

I did as he suggested. It took me a minute or so to get the hang of the thing, but before long I was able to start to "see" stuff.

"All right, Jim," Kenny said. "Tell me what you see."

"OK. First, it's obvious where there are lights turned on. The main house, the lab, and the cottage nearest the shore all have lights on. Their heat patterns really stand out. But you don't need the scope to figure that out. You can just see those. Beyond that, I can tell that there's something under the banyan trees giving out some kind of heat signal. Kenny, what do you think that is?"

"My guess is that that's the gorilla."

"That makes sense," I said. "I think I can see one of the guards, too. He is over on the other shore near the dock. The motor on that golf cart really throws off some heat, and I can also see a glow from what I presume is the guard's body. Anything else you think I ought to look at?

"Jim, why don't you take a closer look at the two cottages, and tell me what you can see?"

"Well, the nearest one has lights on. But I already told you that. Also, I'm seeing a signal from what I presume is the front room, which I'd guess might be a television or some other kind of electronic equipment. Maybe a guard, too. In the rear of the cottage, in what I presume would be the bedroom, I get a less intense signal. But maybe that's coming from a sleeping guard's body."

"Very good! You're really getting the hang of using that thing. Now, what about the other cottage?" he asked.

"I'm not seeing much," I replied. "It's dark, and as far as I can tell, there's no electronics in there. They said it's just a storehouse. That's the way it looks to me."

"Keep looking."

I held the scope as still as I could for close to a minute. Finally, I could see what Kenny was talking about. "Whoa! Kenny, I think I see it. There's just the faintest glow coming from the back room. I can't see any movement. It looks kind of like the signal from that gorilla, but fainter. What do you think it might be?"

"The signal's less intense because of the walls," he explained. "The gorilla is in a cage. It'd be my guess that there's probably someone in that back room. Maybe it's just another guard sleeping. But it could be anything."

"What do you mean, 'anything'?" I asked.

"Well, if the guards don't sleep there, maybe there's someone else in there? Maybe someone is sleeping. Or, who knows, maybe someone's being kept there against their will."

"Damn, Kenny. You just had to say that, didn't you?"

"Sorry. Jim, we know how to get on the island now. You want to go have a closer look at that cottage?" he asked.

"Hell, no! I've already told you that I'm not going on there unless I have to. But I am going to suggest that Mike Collins ought to have a better look around."

"Jim, I don't want to disappoint you, but I don't think the lieutenant has that in mind."

"Yeah, I hear you," I replied. "But maybe this will convince him otherwise. Kenny, I've had enough of this place for tonight. You ready to get out of here?"

"Yeah, Jim, I'm more than ready. I just looked in my cooler, and I've only got a few beers left. You need to get me home ASAP. But first, let me take a piss."

Kenny stepped to the stern, braced himself against the Talon, and let it rip. While I was waiting for him to finish, I called Jill on the cell.

"Are y'all OK?" she asked.

"Yeah, we're fine," I told her. "I just wanted to let you know that we're heading home."

"I appreciate that. I was starting to get worried. By the way, Mike Collins called for you. He said you didn't need to get back tonight, but he'd like to get with you tomorrow. He said he had some news you'd be interested in."

"That's interesting. I've got some news for him, too," I said. "I'll call him in the morning. See you in about an hour."

"Sounds good. Y'all be careful. Love you."

"I love you, too!"

Chapter Thirty-Two

I called Mike Collins in the morning, and we agreed to meet at the Waterfront for lunch. He was sitting in the shade on the back deck, in his usual spot. As I walked toward him, I couldn't help but notice that he looked happy, quite possibly more than just a little bit pleased with himself. He was talking on his cell.

I sat down and waited for him to finish his call. He waved and held up his thumb and finger close together, giving me the signal that he would be done soon. I saw that he was listening, but then I heard him speak to end the call. "Hey, babe. Look, I've got some-one here, and I've got to go. I'll see you tonight. Bye."

As he hung up, I looked him in the eyes, raising one eyebrow in the most questioning manner I could manage.

He laughed. Obviously, he had enjoyed the call.

We shook hands, and I began the necessary interrogation.

"So, Mike, you still on with the chick from the police department?"

I was referring back to a relationship he'd had six months earlier—a relationship I had unintentionally interrupted with an ill-timed early morning phone call.

"No," he replied. "Oh, hell no. That phone call you made was probably one of the best things that ever happened to me. I need to buy you a beer someday to thank you for that."

"OK," I said. "Glad I could help, but—I'll bite—why was that call a good thing?"

"Well, after that she took up with a buddy of mine up in the Charlotte County department. And it's been downhill for him ever since."

"How come?"

"Well, he's absolutely crazy about her," he replied. "But she's got really, really expensive tastes. To keep her happy, I think he's going to have to resign and get a real job. Shit, that could have been me!"

"Glad I could help. How about your new friend? Anyone I know?" I asked.

"She's not from the island. I'm not that crazy. But you've probably seen her—she's the new traffic chick on WINK."

"She's hot."

"Yeah," he said. "She is that, and we're getting along great."

"Is that why you've got that goofy grin on your face?" I asked.

"Probably," he replied. "But that's only one of the good things going on in my life right now. In fact, that's why I wanted to see you. I think we've finally made progress on some of the folks out here who have disappeared."

"That's fantastic. Tell me about it."

"It's all coming from us busting that pill mill operation on the island. We used the records from the clinic to start leaning on some folks a little bit, and as a consequence, we've started to learn some really interesting stuff. For example, I think we may have discovered what happened to the cook from here who disappeared a while back."

"Damn, Mike. That's great. Is he OK?" I asked.

"No. The news for him is not good. Not good at all. In fact, he's dead. At least, I'm pretty sure he's dead. I know I shouldn't let myself get in a good mood about something like this. But it's kind of like finally solving a puzzle—it just feels good. Here's how we think it went down. You know he was a quiet guy, just kept to himself and lived in that old cracker house over on fourth. Not much of a house, and we searched it when he went missing. Didn't find a thing. But when we leaned on one of one of the guys associated with the pill mill, we learned something interesting. The cook, apparently having a lot of time on his hands, had built an extensive meth lab. From what we've learned, he was cooking up all the meth the island needed and delivering it on his bicycle. It was a sweet little operation. My guess is that he was doing it as much for fun, and to relieve the boredom, as for the money. We went back to the house and had a more thorough look. There was nothing in the house, but we found that there was an abandoned lot behind it. The lot looked to be completely covered by a jungle of impenetrable Brazilian peppers. When we had been there before, we had looked around but couldn't find any sign that he might have been in there. But this time, when we looked more closely, we found where the cook had meticulously carved out a nearly invisible crawlway back into the jungle. When we crawled in there, we found where he had cleared out a big enough space for his lab. I guess the guy just really liked to cook. He cooked food at work and meth in his spare time. But eventually, I guess the pill mill guys found out about him and decided to eliminate the competition. They caught him out on Stringfellow one night. Next thing you know, they chained him to his bicycle, weighted it down with some lead plates, and threw him in the pond behind the American Legion. Our divers pulled him out of there yesterday. Or at least, they pulled someone out of there. I'm waiting to hear confirmation if it was him. But I don't think there's any doubt."

"They threw him in the pond behind the Legion?" I asked incredulously.

"Yeah. Can you believe that? Right next to where everybody sits on the patio to smoke."

"Why there? That seems a little too conspicuous, and I wouldn't think that pond would be that deep."

"Actually, you would be wrong," he told me. "That pond is normally about fifteen feet deep. I guess it was dug to provide fill for the building's foundation years ago. And among the locals, it's common knowledge that the pond is deep and can be a good place to dispose of stuff. In fact, about ten years ago, we had to pull a body in a car out of there. This old guy, no family around, got drunk at the bar one night, and when leaving, he put his car in forward instead of reverse and drove right into the pond. He was in there a long time. The only way it was discovered that he was in there was when the level of the pond fell during a drought. And, I guess the drought had caused the water in the pond to get clear, too. As I remember hearing about it, one of the members was out there looking at the pond's resident alligators one day and almost had a heart attack when he saw that car."

"Jeez. Who would have figured that?"

Mike laughed gently and said, "There's never a dull day in my line of work."

"Mike, what about the other guys who have disappeared? What about Tommy, his brother, and the kid with the tattoo? Have you learned anything about them?"

"No. Not yet. But I suspect we will. It's probably all connected with this pill mill stuff in some way. Usually, when they start knocking folks off, they don't stop with just one. I think we'll find them."

"Mike, I appreciate you letting me know about this. I really do. But I don't think that's what happened." I went on to tell him about what Kenny and I had discovered the previous night.

When I finished, I noticed that the smile on the lieutenant's face had gone away, and the twinkle in his eyes had been replaced with a steely cold glare. "Jim, you need to let this go," he snapped. "And you need to stay out of my business. You are about to piss me off. No. Let me correct myself. You have already pissed me off. Royally! I'm sorry I came out here today; it was a clearly a mistake. From this point forward, our friendship is over. Our dealings with each other, should there ever be any in the future, will be strictly professional. And, Mr. Story, if I find out that you or your friends have been trespassing on Dr. Areola's property, I will arrest you and see that you are prosecuted to the fullest extent allowed by Florida statutes. You need to go back to just being a retired old fart. Maybe you ought to take up golf, or shuffleboard, or bridge, or something equally harmless. In fact, why don't you go over to the fucking casino on the reservation with all the other losers? Just go somewhere else, and stay out of my fucking business!"

At that point, the food we had ordered arrived. He stood up, threw a twenty-dollar bill on the table, and stormed out.

The waitress, clearly flustered, didn't know what to say. Finally, she asked, "Should I box that up?"

"Yeah, that would be a good idea," I replied. "Why don't you box both of them up, and bring me the check?"

Chapter Thirty-Three

"How'd that go?" Jill asked, as I walked in the door.

"That was not good," I replied. "Not good at all." I went on to tell her about finding the cook's body and about Lieutenant Collins's reaction to my suggestion that he should go have another look around Little Bokeelia Island.

"I hate to hear that, on both counts," Jill said. "So I guess that's the end of looking for Tommy?" she asked.

"The end, my ass! Just because Mike Collins is impressed with that damn Spanish genius doesn't mean that I am. I want to see what, or who, is in that second cottage. And I've got some friends here who I think will be willing to help me do that. I'm going to start making some phone calls."

"Honey, tell me again what Mike said he'd do to you if you were caught trespassing on that island?" Jill asked. I knew she, in her lighthearted way, was trying to make sure that I wasn't letting anger override common sense. She wanted to make sure that I was thinking this through. However, I also knew that she wasn't totally opposed to the idea. If she had been, she'd have been quite direct in making sure that I understood just how stupid she thought the idea was.

"Oh, he said something about a possible arrest. But that would only happen if we got caught. And I don't intend for that to happen."

"Babe, let me remind you that just because you like to read Randy Wayne White's books, that doesn't qualify you to behave like Doc Ford. The last time you decided to take the law into your own hands, you almost got yourself and a good friend killed."

"Not a problem," I replied. "I'm a lot more qualified than you're giving me credit for. Not only have I read all the books, but I also have spent a lot of time at all three Doc Ford's Rum Bars. As you well know, I've probably eaten my weight in Doc Ford's delicious Yucatan Shrimp. Surely that qualifies me for something?"

Jill sighed deeply. "The only thing that's qualified you for is a larger pants size. Seriously, you need to be careful."

With that out of the way, I took my cell out onto the pool deck and began to make phone calls.

The first call was to Kenny. I knew he'd be up for the plan. The next was to Steve Fairchild. He'd saved my ass in our previous law enforcement adventure, but he'd also almost been killed. I wasn't sure how'd he'd react to another invitation, but he jumped at the opportunity. Finally, I called Terry, our friend in Bokeelia.

All three of these guys were retired, but that didn't mean that they weren't qualified for what I had in mind. Kenny had spent decades building telephone systems in the jungles of South America. There wasn't much that scared him. Steve was a retired

US Army Ranger captain. He'd spent multiple tours in both Iraq and Afghanistan. But, an IED had put an early end to his military career. He'd spent a year at Walter Read getting put back together. But, now, other than the cane he had to rely on to walk with, folks that didn't know him well would be hard pressed to tell that he'd been injured. Terry was a Central Florida redneck. However, that description sells him way too short, and some further explanation is required.

He'd grown up in the Green Swamp, a large, low-lying wetlands area that covered most of the middle part of the state. Even to this day, there's not much there except pastureland and cypress sloughs. His family lived in one of the small towns on the outskirts of this area, and his parents lived normal small-town lives. But for some unknown reason, probably due to some kind of poorly appreciated genetic mutation, Terry loved the swamps. While legend has it that Davy Crocket had killed a bear by the time he was three, that exploit pales in comparison to some of the stuff Terry accomplished as a kid. For example, killing wild boar was, for him, routine. And he'd been able to buy his first truck by capturing rattlesnakes and selling them to a local serpentarium. And a talent with dynamite became obvious early on, as the following story illustrates.

Terry was always a bright kid, but he really wasn't cut out for the rules that went along with school. Still, somehow, despite his lack of application, he was able to make it through high school and thought that he was going to actually graduate. However, on the morning of graduation day, the principal called Terry into his office to inform him that he was one credit short and, consequently, would not be able to take part in that night's ceremony.

As you might expect, Terry was upset. However, perhaps that was for the best, because it turned out that the ceremony was one that few would ever forget. Just as Terry's classmates began to walk across the stage to receive their diplomas, the football field, where the ceremony was taking place, was rocked by a series of explosions beyond the empty visitors' grandstands—explosions that propelled a number of nearby orange trees, trees that had been killed by that winter's freeze, high into the air above those stands. Later investigation determined that a quarter stick of dynamite had likely been placed beneath each tree. However, the perpetrator was never discovered.

As it turned out, the principal had actually been "mistaken" about Terry not having earned enough credits to graduate. Some suspected, and probably rightly so, that the principal had been concerned about whatever prank Terry had planned to liven up the night's event and had used this mistake as a way to protect the ceremony from that prank being pulled. But I'm sure he never anticipated the extent of Terry's revenge. Neither did he anticipate that his grass yard at home would soon succumb to a late-night application of Roundup that occurred shortly after Terry learned that he should have participated in the graduation ceremony after all. As I said, Terry was a Central Florida redneck, but one with very unique qualifications. Talents that I thought just might come in handy.

I'd invited the "team" to come by the house at five that afternoon. Jill had a Matlacha Hookers (the island's female service organization) committee meeting and wouldn't be home until about seven. We gathered around the wicker table that sat alongside the swimming pool. I provided beer and cans of Off. Pool screens keep mosquitoes away, but they are useless against sand gnats (aka no-see-ums). But we were soon both protected and for-tified, and we quickly got down to business.

I brought everyone up to speed on what had transpired, and on Lieutenant Collins's warning. Kenny briefed the group on the results of our exploration using the night vision goggles. Soon we began formulating a plan.

Steve, being the pro that he was, took the lead. "So, Jim, what specifically is the objective for this mission?"

"Specifically, I want to get on the island to determine if any-one is being held hostage in that second cottage. And, if possible, I want to see what's in the rest of the laboratory; the rear section that they told Collins hadn't been built out. Call me a skeptic, but I don't buy that. There's something else in that part of the building, and I'd like to know what it is."

As we pondered that, a mullet jumped, heading down the canal. We all turned to watch while he executed a series of five consecutive leaps. Maybe something was after him. Or maybe he was simply just jumping for joy. I hoped it was the latter. And I couldn't help but wonder whether our group wasn't somehow like that mullet. Was there something evil and threatening swim-ming in our waters, or were we just bored and in need of some-thing exciting to do?

Steve brought us back to the task at hand. "It looks to me like this operation has a number of key elements. Some of the things we'll need to consider are timing, logistics, insertion of the search party, protection of the search party while it carries out its mission, extraction of the search party if the mission is successful, and, of course, contingency planning in case the mission doesn't go as planned. Let's take them one by one."

I could see at this point that Kenny had leaned forward, obviously getting into the planning. Terry, on the other hand, had sat back in his chair and appeared to just be staring off at a Great Egret that was sunning itself on top of the boathouse. I also noticed that we weren't drinking our beers.

Steve asked, "Jim, when do you have in mind for doing this?"

"I want to do it as soon as possible. If Tommy or anyone else is being held in that place, we need to get them out."

Steve answered, "How about tomorrow night? The weather's going to be good, the moon's full, and there'll be a flood tide coming in all night. Y'all OK with that?"

Everyone answered in the affirmative.

"OK, how about transportation?" Steve continued.

I replied, "Kenny and me on my boat. How about you and Terry on his boat? It's up in Bokeelia."

Steve answered, "I like it. Y'all OK with that?"

Everyone mumbled, "Yeah."

"What time do we want to do the insertion?" I asked.

Steve replied, "Sometime after midnight would be my suggestion. Maybe around two o'clock. How's everyone feel about that?"

"Two o'clock in the morning?" Kenny exclaimed. "The last time I was awake that late, or is it up that early, I was…hell, I don't know that I've ever been awake at two o'clock in the morning!"

"Exactly!" Steve answered. "Nobody ever expects anything to happen at that time of day. Y'all OK with that?"

Kenny and I answered yes. Terry continued to stare.

"OK. Now, let's discuss the insertion phase of the operation. What are y'all thinking? First, who's going to be in the landing party?" Steve asked.

I spoke up. "I'm the only one going ashore. I don't want anyone else having to deal with a potential trespassing charge from the sheriff. And besides, one person should be able to quickly take a look at both the cottage and the lab. I'm thinking that Kenny can help me get near that boathouse, and then I'll swim over to the ladder. Y'all can create a distraction on the other side of the island. As soon as the guards are over there, trying to find out what's going on, I'll climb the ladder, run over to the cottage, and take a look inside. If that goes well, I'll see what I can find over at the lab. If y'all can keep the guards busy for five minutes, I should be able to do both of those things and be back in the water and on the way to rendezvous with Kenny. As soon as I'm back onboard, we'll call you on the cell, and y'all can get the hell back to Bokeelia. How does that sound?"

At this point, Terry finally spoke up. "I think it's the right idea. I like the idea of creating a distraction. And, as you know, I'm good at blowing shit up. But I think the wrong guy's going ashore. No offense, Jim, but you're a fat, fucking retired banker. When's the last time you tried to sneak around in the dark? I think I ought to be the one going ashore. Hell, that's the kind of thing I do for fun."

I looked Terry in the eyes. I knew he was serious, and I knew what he had suggested had merit. There could be no question but that he would be better on the ground than me. However, I couldn't let that happen. "Terry, you're right, of course. But I can't agree to that. I'm not going to expose you to that kind of risk. Besides, if something should go wrong, I'm going to need all of y'all to help get me out."

Terry said nothing and returned to staring off in the direction of the canal. This time I noticed he was looking at the flock of ibis that had taken up residence on the edge of the dock.

"Speaking of trouble," Steve asked, "are we going to be armed?"

I spoke up, "I don't think we should be. There's no way in hell that we could stand up to those guys in a gunfight, and besides, us having weapons would just give them the excuse to kill us. Everybody agree? No guns."

No one objected.

Steve spoke next, "OK. How does this play out? Let's talk it through. First, assuming all goes well and you're back on the boat, then we'll talk on the cell, and everybody goes home? Is that right?"

"It depends on what I find," I said.

"What do you mean?" Kenny asked.

"Assume that they've got somebody held up in that cottage. Should I try to get him out? Or should I just return to the boat and call the sheriff?"

Everyone looked at each other. Nobody said anything. Finally, Terry made a fist and stuck his right thumb out, then gave the baseball ump's signal for "you're out." He followed up by saying, "Jim, you need to get the hell out of there and let the sheriff take care of springing the guy."

"I agree," I said. "I'll get out—unless the guy's in some kind of eminent danger. If the plan needs to change, I'll have my cell with me, and I'll let you know."

"All right with me," Steve replied. "Now, let's talk about what we'll do if things *don't* go according to plan. What if, for example, the guards catch you and call the sheriff?"

At that point, Terry laughed and said, "I don't know about you guys, but if that happens, I'm getting the hell out of there!"

Everyone laughed, but then Kenny asked, "But what if Jim's captured and they *don't* call the sheriff? Besides, how are we supposed to know if they've called the sheriff or not?"

"Good point," Terry replied. "Steve, what do you think?"

"I would suggest that if we see Jim being apprehended, we should call the sheriff ourselves and throw ourselves on the mercy of the court. Actually, if that should happen, we'll need to keep a close eye on what they're doing with Jim and play it by ear. If it looks like it's getting serious, we'll need to intervene."

"No guns?" Terry asked.

"No guns," I replied.

"Sounds like fun," Terry said.

I just looked at him and shook my head. I knew that it sounded like he was trying to be funny, but I knew better. He meant it.

To change the subject, Steve asked, "What have we forgotten?"

I spoke up. "How are y'all going to distract the guards?"

Terry replied, "Let me worry about that. That way it'll be a surprise for everyone. I think I'll go fishing over there in the morning, just to get a look around."

"OK, Terry," I replied. "Just don't let them get a good look at you. I don't want them to know that any of you are involved. And, guys, remember one thing. We don't know if there's anything fishy out there or not. So we can't just go destroying stuff." At this point I was looking straight into Terry's eyes. "If it turns out that everything's on the up and up, and we've blown up some property, then not only will we have to worry about time in the county jail, but we'll also have a big bill for restitution."

THE CUT BAIT MURDERS

Terry looked back at me and, for a time, didn't say anything. Finally, he said one word: "Shit." He then returned to staring at the ripples made in the canal by a school of passing mullet.

Chapter Thirty-Four

The guys left. Jill came home a little after seven thirty.

"Hey, babe! How'd your meeting go?" I asked.

"It was great. We got a lot done. I think the fishing derby's going to be bigger this year than ever."

"Fishing derby? Is this like a contest where guys go out in teams to see who can catch the biggest fish?" I asked.

"No. That may be part of it, but the main event is for elementary-aged school kids. We give them fully rigged rods and reels and some bait, and, with a little supervision, we let them fish off the dock of the old fish house in Matlacha. All the kids love it. There's also a huge silent auction, food, drinks, bands, you name it. Last year we raised over twenty thousand dollars for the elementary school, and this year is going to be more than that."

"Wow! I had no idea. That's a lot of money, and it sounds like fun. The Hookers are really a great organization, and they do a lot of good on the island. And I really love the name," I said.

"Yeah," Jill replied. "It is a great group. I'm really glad that I'm involved. And we all love the name. What lady, deep down, doesn't really want to be able to say, at one time or another, that she is a hooker?"

I laughed. "I love telling people, when they ask what my wife does, that she's a hooker!"

Jill gave me the evil eye and said, "I bet you do!"

Not to be deterred, I ventured on. "I love your initiation rite for new members. I think it was just a stroke of genius on the part of whoever came up with the idea of putting a garland of flowers around the new member's neck and proclaim that they have just been 'lei'd'! And what is it that y'all call the leader of your group?"

"She's the 'madam,' of course."

"Of course, she is. How could I have forgotten that? You guys are something else."

Jill then asked, "How did your meeting go?"

"It was good, too. All the guys are going to go with me tomorrow night. They're going to try to get me on the island about two o'clock in the morning, so that I can have a look around."

"Honey, do you think that's really a good idea?" Jill asked.

"Probably not. But somebody's got to do it. Now what's for dinner?" I asked.

"That's a hell of a way to change the subject," Jill responded. "But now that you mention it, I've got nothing laid out, no pun intended. What would you think about going down to Woody's?"

Woody's was my favorite restaurant and bar in town. And that night, Woody's was packed. At first it looked as though we wouldn't be able to find seats in the main room, but just as we started to head toward the deck out back, we noticed two guys leaving the bar, so we took their places. As we sat down, we noticed that to our right was one of the bar's regulars, a friend of ours, a guy named Mack. He was supposedly a retired fishing guide—but although he may have been retired, he was still a full-time character. He wore his hair down to his waist, usually in a braid. On top of his head, he always wore a beat-up cowboy hat, complete with an embroidered band that looked like it was stitched by a talented Seminole seamstress. And on that band he'd arranged a display of large alligator incisors. They were about two to three inches long and bleached white. It was an impressive piece of headwear, and Mack was very proud of it.

We chatted awhile, had some drinks, and ordered our meals. All the while, Rip, the open mike night MC, was trying to ride herd on his charges. They, on the other hand, encouraged by suggestions from some of the bar's over served patrons, kept trying to veer off the reservation. It was promising to be a fun evening.

Later, as we were finishing our dinners, and after the consumption of considerably more alcohol by most of the establishment's guests, I noticed one of the elderly ladies at a nearby table get up and walk over to talk with Mack. I couldn't hear what they were saying, but at first it looked like Mack was getting a little indignant. After a minute or so, I saw him start to laugh; then he took off his hat and held it down where the lady could take a better look at the band. I could see them engage in what looked to be a pretty earnest dialogue before the lady finally started to laugh as well. Then she stood up on her tiptoes, put the hat back on Mack's head, and gave him a kiss on the cheek before tottering back to the group at her table. When she got there, I could see all her other tablemates listening intently as she tried to explain something.

I could see their eyes getting big before, they too, broke out in laughter. With that, I couldn't resist asking Mack what he and the little old dear had talked about.

"Jim," he said, laughing, "you're not going to believe this. She came over to ask me why I was wearing—and I swear I'm not making this up—she asked me why I was wearing tampon penetrators on my hat!"

"Tampon penetrators? What the hell are those?"

"Oh, you know those plastic shells things that tampons come in to help the ladies insert the tampons. I swear that I'm telling the truth, that's what she asked me. I guess she'd never seen an alligator's tooth before."

After I could control my own laughter, I asked Mack, "So what'd you tell her?"

"Well," he replied, "I carefully explained to her that they were hollow and were associated with females, but they were not, in fact, made out of plastic. I let her look at them closely, but she didn't have any idea what they were. Finally, I told her that they were eye teeth that I had personally taken from the mouths of alligators. I went on to let her down easy, telling her that I could easily understand why she had been confused, since they had, in fact, all been pulled from the jaws of female alligators."

"You told her you had pulled them from the mouths of gators? Did you ever tell her that you'd actually pulled them from the skulls of long-dead gators out at your friend's gator farm?"

"Well, no. I didn't actually get into that. Just didn't see that it would add to the story."

"Yeah," I said. "I can see your point. So, what did she say?"

"Well, at first, I think she thought I might have been pulling her leg. But after I let her look at those teeth up close, I think she finally believed me. And I've noticed now that all her girlfriends at the table are looking at me with quite a bit more interest than they were before."

I laughed. "I've noticed that you usually have that effect on women. Now I know why."

"Whatever it takes, Jim. Whatever it takes." With that, he left some bills on the bar and headed for the door.

We weren't far behind.

Chapter Thirty-Five

The next morning the phone rang early. It was Kenny calling.

"Hey, buddy," I said. "What's up?"

"Jim, I've got a little issue that's come up and want to run it by you."

"You're not getting cold feet about tonight, are you?" I asked.

"Well, I guess you could say that I am getting cold feet, but not about what we're planning up at Little Bokeelia."

"Kenny, what the hell are you talking about? If not that, what are you scared of?"

"Jim, I was down at Froggy's last night, and there were two ladies down there, Roxie and Georgia—do you know them?"

"Kenny, you know I know them. They're great ladies, and everybody in town knows them. What did they do to you that's got you so upset?"

"Damn it, Jim. They got me so confused, you know how they are—they're hard to say no to. Anyway, after a while I just couldn't figure out what to say."

"Kenny, what the hell are you talking about? Are you OK? What did they do to you? And, what does that have to do with tonight?" I asked.

"Jim...." I could hear him hesitate, and I knew that he was having trouble getting something out. I didn't let him off the hook; I just kept quiet and waited for him to get to the point.

"Damn, it Jim, they are trying to fix me up with this new lady in town, and they want me to come to dinner tonight," he said finally.

"Kenny, that's great."

"So you think I ought to go?"

"That depends," I said.

"Depends? Depends on what?" Kenny asked.

"Have you met this lady? What's she like? What does she look like?"

"Well, they introduced us last night, but we only just said hello."

"And...?" I prodded.

"Well, she seemed nice, and she looked...cute!" he replied.

With that, I couldn't contain myself any longer and burst out laughing. "Kenny, you old fart, how old are you?"

"Jim, you know that I'm one year older than you. What's that got to do with anything?"

"Kenny, if someone as old as you is calling a lady 'cute,' then I'm pretty sure that you're really in a bunch of trouble," I told him.

"So, you don't think I should go to dinner?" he asked.

"Oh, hell no! You've got to go. Those ladies would rip you up from one side to the other if you turned them down. And besides, it'll help to keep you awake—and, hopefully, relatively sober—until it's time for us to head north. Just be at my house at midnight. But if you don't show up, I'll understand why."

"I'll see you then," Kenny said.

"Maybe," I laughed. We hung up.

Next, I called Steve. He was still on for later. He'd already talked with Terry, and they were planning to be on scene off the north shore of the island at one forty-five. I told him that sounded perfect and that we'd stay in touch by cell. We were good to go.

Later in the morning, Jill and I took the boat over to Sanibel Marina and fueled it up. While we were there, we had lunch at Grandma Dot's, a nice little place that adjoined the marina and served great food. Over lunch I told Jill about my conversation with Kenny.

She laughed and said, "Oh, I already know all about that. Roxie told me that they were going to do that a couple of days ago."

I looked at her, feeling more than slightly stupid, and finally managed to say, "You knew?"

"Of course. They've been planning this for a while. It's all been arranged."

"What do you mean, 'it's all been arranged'?" I asked.

"Well, you know, just getting them together," she replied.

"Do you know this lady?" I asked.

"Of course I do. She's great. I really like her."

"She's new in town?" I asked.

"Relatively. I think she and her sister have owned a part-time place here for quite some time. But she just moved here full time when she retired a couple of months ago."

"Where'd she move from, and what'd she used to do?"

"I think she lived somewhere up near DC, and, from what I understand, she had some kind of government job. But that's all I know. That, and that's she's very nice, and that I like her."

"Kenny said he thought she was cute," I added.

Hearing that, Jill's face lit up. I suspected that she would be sharing that tidbit of information shortly among her network of local conspirators.

The rest of the day passed pleasantly. I spent some time organizing myself and my equipment for the evening. Never having played the role of secret agent before, I took some time trying to figure out what I should wear. I figured that my black, long-sleeved T-shirt, the one with the pirate logo on the front, would be appropriate for the mission. To cover my legs, I decided to wear a pair of black exercise leggings that were leftover from when I used to run during the winter up in Birmingham. To cover my feet I selected black water shoes that I had bought years ago when I had tried, unsuccessfully, to learn to scuba dive. My ears just wouldn't take it. For my head, I was ecstatic to remember the black Doc Ford baseball cap I'd bought over in Fort Myers Beach. I thought it would look good if I wore it backward. I put on my ensemble and walked out into the living room to model it for Jill. I wasn't reassured when she burst out laughing.

"Wait a minute! What are you laughing at?" I asked. "Haven't you ever seen a secret agent before?"

"Oh, honey, I'm sorry," she said, still laughing. "I guess for a minute I thought you had put on a Shamu costume." With that, she began to laugh so hard that she fell over onto her side on the couch.

I was not amused. "Hey, I didn't make fun of you last year for Halloween when you dressed up with the girls like Gene Simmons in Kiss."

"Yeah. But I was hot! And, I know that you know it," she replied.

"How do you know that?" I asked.

"Think about it, babe. And think back on how much trouble you had with that spiked dog collar!"

"Oh, yeah. You *were* pretty hot. But I guess you're not getting the same vibe from this outfit, huh?"

"I guess I'm just really not that into overweight orcas," she said. With that, she fell over laughing again.

"OK, OK! I get your point." Trying to not become too insulted, I decided to change the subject. "Do you have any of the black face paint left over from your Kiss days?"

"Oh, honey, I'm sorry," Jill said. "I didn't mean to hurt your feelings. I do have some of it upstairs."

She left to retrieve it. I could hear her laughing all the way. I deduced from her reaction that my outfit might not actually instill quite the degree of fear that I had hoped. Still, it would have to do. It was all I had.

We had an early dinner around seven, watching, as was our custom, *Wheel of Fortune* and *Jeopardy*. Then, having established once again the relatively shameful level of my IQ, we debated what to watch next. But once we had deduced that there was nothing on television more stimulating to watch than *Moonshiners*, I decided to try to get a few hours' sleep. I left Jill with *Tickle* and went upstairs. To my surprise, I must have been able to drop off, because the next thing I was aware of was being awakened by Jill gently shaking me, saying, "Babe, you better wake up. It's almost time for Kenny to show up."

I jumped up, showered, put on my costume and my face, and took the rest of my stuff downstairs. Jill had fixed some sandwiches for us to take along and put on a pot of coffee. While I was waiting on Kenny, I took the boat off the lift and made sure, once again, that it was in order. A few minutes after twelve, we saw Kenny pull into the driveway. I noticed, as he walked up the stairs, that he looked sober. I also noticed that he had also made an attempt at a blackout ensemble, but he had pulled his off a little more successfully—black sweater, black watch cap, black jeans, and black sneakers. I also thought I noticed him try to stifle a grin when he got a look at me.

Not wanting to give him the chance to start laughing, I asked him, "Hey, Kenny, how was your evening?" I noticed a strange look in his eyes. I couldn't make it out. It could have been joy or possibly a mild case of bewilderment. Probably, I guessed, some of both.

"Jim, it was fun. We really had a good time."

"So, you liked the lady?" I asked.

"Yeah. I did. She's really nice, and I think she's, you know, I think she's…."

With that, I interrupted, "I know, you think she's cute!"

"Now, damn it, Jim. Don't you start. Are we ready to go?"

"Yeah. How about you? Are you sober?" I asked, figuring that Roxie and Georgia had done their best to loosen him up.

"Yeah, I'm fine. I only had a couple of glasses of wine, you know, just to be polite. So, I'm in good shape," he told me.

"Well, I've always thought that it was good policy to not get stewed on the first date," I said. "You usually make a better impression that way."

"Damn it, Jim, it wasn't a date," he protested. "Just a group of friends having dinner."

I laughed and said, "Whatever. You want a cup of coffee?"

Ten minutes later we were ready to go. I gave Jill a hug and a kiss, and then we hugged again—this time with feeling.

"All right, babe. We've got to go," I said. "Don't wait up. I'll see you in the morning."

"Wrong! Make sure you wake me up when you get back. Love you."

"I love you, too."

With that, we all walked down to the dock. Kenny and I climbed onboard. As soon as we had settled our stuff, I twisted the key to the engine, which quietly came to life. We brought the dock lines onboard. Just before I put the boat in gear, I looked one more time at Jill. I gave her my biggest smile and winked, but I noticed that she wasn't smiling.

With that, we were off.

Chapter Thirty-Six

At one thirty, I quietly slipped over the side of the boat and into the black waters of the bay south of Little Bokeelia. We had positioned the boat to look as if we were fishing the mangroves, possibly for snook. My plan was to paddle over to the ladder that led up the island's boathouse and wait to hear the distraction that Steve and Terry had planned. Then, as soon as the guards had reacted to that and gone to explore, I would climb the ladder and head ashore.

The night was dark. A thin layer of stratus obscured the moon and the stars—a perfect night for staying hidden. I couldn't help but think, just for a moment, that it might also be a perfect night for sharks to be feeding. But I tried to put that thought out of my mind as I began to slowly, quietly swim toward the island. I had on a set of dive fins and had positioned a dive mask and snorkel on the top of my head. However, I decided to not put those on my face, preferring instead to keep my head above water so I could keep watch on what was happening on the island. Not that there was that much to see. I could tell that there were lights burning over the doors of both cottages, as well on both ends of the laboratory. I also noticed that there was a single light burning over the door of the boathouse. I hadn't counted on that. But other than that, nothing seemed to be unusual. I had to assume that somewhere, there was at least one guard, sitting on a golf cart and keeping a careful watch. But Kenny, using the night vision scope, had not been able to make out where. I swam as quietly as I could, using a sidestroke, making sure that the only part of me sticking out of the water was my head.

Swimming in the sound, even in the daylight, is not for the faint of heart. The water there is home to a huge variety of marine creatures, all of whom seem to be engaged in a constant struggle to both eat and avoid being eaten. I'm not really sure where a semi-obese, slowly swimming human fits in that food chain, but I was fairly certain that even as I swam, there was at least one large creature waiting in the water, watching and trying to figure that question out. I just hoped it wasn't a bull shark that was mulling this thought over. There is no doubt that bull sharks sit at the top of the sound's food chain. They're big, fast, and strong and have a mouthful of sizeable, razor-sharp teeth. In addition, they're aggressive and mean as hell. I know that most creatures in the sound aren't that interested in making a meal out of any randomly passing *homo sapiens*, but bull sharks apparently didn't get the memo. They'd just as soon snack on a person's leg and foot as they would on a mackerel. And as if that wasn't bad enough, I couldn't help but remember that they loved to feed at night in the sound's shallow flats.

I tried my best to put these thoughts on the back burner, but every time I heard the splash from a jumping mullet, I couldn't help but shiver, wondering what might have been chasing it. Once or twice I heard more prolonged thrashing and crashing that seemed to come from the shallows near the shore. I presumed these sounds were probably made by hungry snook or redfish chasing bait, but each time I also involuntarily flashed back to the many times I had seen large sharks feeding in water less than a foot deep. *Crap*. It was dark. All I could do was keep swimming, slowly pulling myself in the direction of the boathouse.

I judged that I had been in the water for maybe twenty minutes. I was probably within fifty yards of the boathouse. I knew from earlier explorations of the area that the water here, relative to other parts of the bayou, was pretty deep. I'd have guessed that with the night's tide, it was maybe eight feet deep. I stopped swimming for a moment, treading water to rest. I knew that I had plenty of time to get to the ladder before the fireworks were scheduled to go off. That was when I felt the bump.

It hadn't been a hard hit—more like an exploratory glance. But I hadn't imagined it. Something was definitely in the water with me. Something large...and something that was definitely interested in me. The shock of that encounter definitely tested the quality of the repairs my heart surgeon had performed a few years previously. He must have done a great job. And, despite the fear and the rush of adrenalin that that fear had produced, I somehow managed to stay silent. However, I wasn't sure that if whatever had hit me came back, I would be able to do that again. In fact, I was actually hoping that if it came back, I would somehow be able to start running on top of the water. I had no doubt that I could make it all the way to the dock. Then I felt the swirl.

Whatever it was, it was still swimming near me. No more than a few feet. It seemed like it was staying close, almost as if it was stalking me. I debated what to do. Should I stay still and wait to be eaten? Or should I swim for the dock and maybe scare the creature off? Or would swimming just make it mad and entice it to strike? I had just decided that the odds were in favor of swimming when I heard the sound.

Pusssssssssssssss.

I don't think I've ever been happier in my life than when I heard that manatee breathe. I almost wanted to swim over and kiss it. Instead, I resumed stroking for the boathouse's ladder. A few minutes later I was holding on to it. Only then did I notice how rapidly I was breathing and how loudly my heart was pounding. Apparently, the encounter with the manatee had done a number on me. Or maybe it was just the anticipation about what was to come.

To calm down, I leaned backward and floated on my back, keeping a loose grip on the ladder with one hand. I noticed, as I looked up toward the sky, that the clouds had thinned, and the moon was starting to shine through. *Great!* Just what I needed. So much for being invisible in the dark. I took a deep breath and returned to the job at hand. I removed the mask, snorkel, and fins and quietly placed them on the dock. And waited. And listened.

After a minute or so, I could make out a few sounds. Coming from the direction of the cottage nearest the water was the unmistakable noise of gentle snoring. Clearly, there was at least one guard sleeping there. I could also occasionally make out what sounded like music, coming from the direction of the path near the laboratory. I tried to pay attention but finally concluded that it was probably just a guard on a golf cart, listening to a radio. Just a guy trying to kill time and stay awake on a long shift, guarding a quiet island during the middle of the night. But that island wasn't going to stay quiet long.

Chapter Thirty-Seven

Thirty seconds later, two huge explosions shattered the island's quiet. Those blasts were followed immediately by the sight of twin fires burning at the location of the blasts, leaping tall into the sky. No question, it was a hell of a distraction. But I had known all along that I could count on Terry and Steve to hold up their end of the deal.

I pulled myself up onto the dock almost before whatever had been blown up into the air had returned to the earth. And then I watched and listened. I heard what sounded like curses coming from the direction of the guard; then I heard his golf cart start and saw its lights come on. I also noticed lights turn on in the front room of the first cottage. Soon, the golf cart was heading in the direction of one of the blasts. I waited to see what was going to happen in the cottage. I could hear sounds of what I assumed was a guard getting dressed and strapping on gear and weapons. Soon I saw a darkly clad figure come out of the door and climb into the other golf cart. As the driver backed out, I could hear the sounds of rounds being racked into the breach of a gun. As this driver screeched off toward the island's eastern tip, I knew that he was serious. Soon that cart was at least a quarter of a mile away, heading quickly in the direction of the second blast. I could see flames still burning on both the northeastern and eastern tips of the island. Showtime.

I walked toward the cottages. I know that Doc Ford would have run, but my running days were long past. Still, it didn't take me long to cover the hundred yards or so that I needed to cross. As much as possible, I tried to stay out of the semicircles of light that radiated from the burning bulbs over each of the cottages doors. Soon, I slid beside the southern wall of the cottage nearest the water. It was dark there. I paused for a couple of seconds, hearing nothing but the sound of my own labored breathing. Then I peeked around the corner and took a quick glance at the door of the cottage before returning to the security of the darkness. I quickly tried to process what I had seen. Closed screen door; lights on; no sign of anyone—but I'd not been able to see inside the back room of the cottage. Hopefully, the third guard was still sleeping there. I'd also noticed, as I had expected, a heavy, whitewashed wooden door swung back against the front wall of the cottage, apparently held in position by some type of hook. I had expected to see this because I knew that these types of old cracker structures on the islands usually had strong, solid doors that could be swung shut and locked from the outside, serving to provide both shelter from hurricane winds and security from local marauders during the long, hot summer months when their owners returned to their homes in the north.

Another peek around the corner confirmed this, and it also confirmed that both the hook and hasp by which the door could be locked by padlock were in place. With that assurance, I stepped around the corner, unhooked the door, and eased it shut. I didn't have a padlock with me, but I had brought along a supply of heavy-duty black zip ties. I closed the hasp, slid one of the zip ties into, and around, the hook, and pulled it tight. There was no way, if there were people still inside, that they were going to come out that front door.

I let out a deep sigh. I'm not sure that I had actually breathed since I'd gotten next to the cottage. Now, with that door locked, I felt a little more comfortable. I paused to listen and to look, trying to decipher what was going on across the island. But there really wasn't much to either see or hear. I eased around the opposite corner of the cottage that I had been hiding behind. Once I was again in the dark. I quietly walked to the side of the other cottage, maybe forty feet away. By now, I was feeling a little bit more at ease. I stuck my head into the light, and studied the front door of that building. This time the heavy wooden door was closed, and locked with what looked like a heavy-duty padlock. No way that I could open that door.

I was disappointed, but not surprised. Mike Collins had mentioned that the door had been locked when he was being shown around. Still, I guess I was hoping that, with the element of surprise on my side, the door might have been open so that I could stroll right through it to see what—or who—was inside. But being this close, I couldn't just give up. I eased down the side of the cottage, working my way toward the back of the house. I noticed that there was a window on the side of the front room, but it was closed and covered with a set of heavy, locked shutters. I tried to get my fingers under the edge of the shutters to hopefully pull them away far enough for me to get a glimpse inside. However, they were neatly recessed into the window's sill, and there was no way to get a grip with my fingers. Possibly, if I had a pry bar with me, I could have done it. But I didn't have one, so I moved on around to the back of the house where, to my surprise, I found another door. This time there was no exterior shutter, just a wooden door, hung to swing to the inside and locked with a dead bolt.

I gave the exterior knob a twist, but it, too, was locked. Finally, in desperation, I pushed against the top corner of the door on the side away from the hinges. I could feel it give a little, but not enough to see inside. Nevertheless, I was encouraged enough with that success to try the same with the bottom corner, this time using my foot to apply pressure. And this time, given the added weight and leverage this approach provided, the corner moved inward enough to provide a gap against the door's sill. Of course, there was no way that I could see through that gap, as it was down near floor level. But at least it was something.

I removed my foot and turned around to lean against the back of the house to rest and gather my thoughts. As I did, I noticed that the cottage sat beneath a couple of what, in silhouette against the moon-lit sky, appeared to be cabbage palms. And lying on the ground underneath, I noticed a frond that one of the trees had recently discarded. I picked it up. Soon I had a plan.

Using the filet knife that I had strapped onto my dive belt, I trimmed the fan end of the frond away from the stalk. Soon the stalk was thin enough to be slid into the gap in the door. And, then, once it was inside, it was easy enough to wedge it further along and use it to pry open the door an inch or so. Just enough for me, lying on the ground and using the small, waterproof pen light that I had brought with me, to see inside the room. The little that I could see was enough to confirm my fears.

The back of this cottage was not, as Mike Collins had been told, being used to store supplies. At least not to store supplies in the conventional sense. Instead, I could see what looked like a hospital bed, several stands that were holding drip bags, and what looked like the types of monitors I remembered seeing when I was doing sheet time in the cardiac ward. From what I could tell, those drip bags and monitors appeared to be operational and hooked up to someone lying in that bed. But I couldn't tell who it was—and I badly wanted to know.

So I gave the palm branch as strong a pull as I could manage. The door opened another inch or so, and for a moment, I thought it was going to pull away enough from the frame that held the lock. But instead, just as I appeared to be on the verge of success, the damn frond broke.

When it did, I fell backward, falling flat on my ass. That pissed me off. I jumped up and used all my strength to throw my shoulder at the door, just like we've all seen them do on television a hundred times. But this door must not have been made out of the same stuff that they use on TV. I soon learned that doors made out of hundred-year-old cypress don't break easily. I wasn't so sure, however, about my shoulder. I tried one more time though, admittedly, with a little less enthusiasm on the second attempt. With that I gave up and decided to move on to my second mission: exploring the portion of the lab building that was supposedly unfinished.

By now, the moon was bright enough that I could see to walk along the stone pathway that ran between the cottages and the laboratory. As I approached the lab, I moved off of the path, and hid behind a bordering banyan. I had no way of knowing whether it was one of the trees planted by Thomas Edison or not. Whoever had planted it, at that moment I was grateful for the cover it provided. The only thing I knew for sure was that I needed to see what was inside that lab, while I still had the chance.

I quickly ran (adrenalin is a powerful thing) the remaining ten yards toward the rear of the lab. Once I reached it, I took a good look around. There were shutters covering all the windows, and there was no light leaking through. The only light came from the bare bulb that burned over the lab building's back door. Having nothing better to do, I decided to try the knob on the door, just to see if it would open. Honestly, I never expected the knob to turn. And I certainly never, ever expected that door to open. But somehow, after I had eased it quietly open enough to get just a quick glimpse of what was inside, I was somehow not surprised by what I saw. The room was bathed in the brightest lights you can imagine, and my eyes were dazzled. But soon I could make out what appeared to be the inside of a fully equipped hospital operating room, and in the middle of the room was what appeared to be the masked and robed figure of a surgeon bending over, peering into, and doing something with his hands inside the chest cavity of a human body.

But then the lights went out. Or, more accurately, then *my* lights went out!

Chapter Thirty-Eight

"Steve, this is Kenny. We've got a problem."

"What do you mean, we've got a problem?" Steve answered on his cell.

"I'm pretty sure those bastards have grabbed Jim," Kenny said.

For a moment, Kenny didn't hear an answer. Finally, in a calm but terse voice, Steve asked, "Why do you think they've grabbed Jim?"

"Steve, I...I don't know for sure, but I believe...I saw them do it on my...night scope." Kenny was starting to gasp as his COPD kicked in.

"Exactly what did you see?"

"I was keeping an eye on Jim the whole time he was on the island. I...I think he might have found something in the cottage, but he'd just...he'd moved on toward the lab. He hid behind a... behind a tree for a couple of minutes. Then he opened the door, and...he stuck his head inside the back door of the lab. I couldn't see much...because there was so much light when...when he opened the door. But I…I guess the other guy must have…must have gotten there first."

"Take it easy, Kenny. Slow down and take a couple of breaths," Steve said.

Kenny did as instructed, pausing for a couple of beats before resuming the story.

"Next think I know, it looks like Jim's flat on the ground—at least I assume it was Jim, and somebody's dragging him back to the second cottage. Then they both…both disappeared inside."

"Shit!" Steve replied. "They've got him, all right."

"Oh my God! Oh my God!" Kenny said. He often tended to repeat himself whenever he got excited. "Steve, now what do we do?"

"Kenny, the first thing you do is to call Mike Collins and tell him what's going on. You've got his number right? You call him and get him and his guys out here. Get them out here, like right now! While you're doing that, Terry and I will talk and come up with a plan. We'll call you back in a couple of minutes."

"OK, OK," Kenny replied.

Several minutes later, Kenny's phone buzzed. It was Steve calling back.

"Did you get in touch with Collins?" Steve asked.

"Yeah. He wasn't very happy, but…I told him what was going on," Kenny replied.

"I don't give a fuck if he was happy or not. Is he on his way?" Steve asked.

"Yeah. But the county's chopper is out of commission again. So it's going to take them a while to get here."

"Damn," Steve responded. "Well, in that case, I guess it's up to us. Kenny, you stay where you are and keep an eye on that cottage with your scope. Whatever you do, don't lose track of Jim. Terry and I are going to try to take care of the guards. I'll call you if I need you. If you see anything going on, text both of us."

With that, Steve ended the call.

"Terry, are you ready to go?" Steve asked.

"I'm ready when you are."

"Do you have the stuff you need?"

Terry answered, "Think so. Got some dock lines, some zip ties, and a shark bat. You got your stuff?"

"Yep. Got my cane, some duct tape, and fifty yards of fishing leader. Should be more than enough to get the job done."

"OK," Terry responded and silently lowered himself off the side of the boat into the inky black water. The last Steve saw before the darkness became too thick, Terry was silently stroking toward the inflatable that was moored alongside the dock on that side of the island.

Steve continued to sit for a few minutes. As he waited he could hear the guards talking on their radios. It sounded as if there was still one guard near where each of the explosions had taken place. He guessed they were simply watching and waiting. He also guessed that there was another standing by in, or near, the guardhouse. He knew they believed that they were ready for whatever might happen next. Little did they know....

Chapter Thirty-Nine

Terry had volunteered to immobilize the guard boat and then to deal with the guard on the northeastern leg of the island. They hadn't gone into many details, but Steve guessed, from what Terry had told him earlier about how he trapped wild hogs, that he wouldn't have a problem dealing with the guard. The plan they had put together was really not much more than trying to buy as much time as they could, trying to prevent any harm from coming to Jim, while hoping the sheriff would arrive before things got too serious. They'd mutually agreed that the seizure of Jim had released them from their previous pledge to not cause any damage to property or persons.

For his part, Steve planned to quietly move the boat toward the eastern end of the island, wade ashore somewhere between the power plant and the buildings at the center of the island, and try to delay things as much as possible. He knew that the guard on that end of the island would be able to keep track of the boat by its engine noise, even if he made as little sound as possible, so he planned to use that to his advantage. For starters, he turned on the boat's nav lights. He wanted the guard to be able to see where the boat was. Once it was near shore, he popped the boat into gear to create some forward momentum, then pulled it back into neutral, leaving the engine running. Then he quietly dropped over the side, taking his cane and other equipment with him. He knew that, in the still waters of the bayou, the boat would drift forward at least a hundred yards and that the sound of the engine, along with the nav lights, would focus the guard's attention on that spot. As he quietly crawled ashore and headed inland toward the coconut palms that lined the cart path, he could tell that the plan had worked. The guard was talking in an animated fashion on his radio, and in the intermittent glow from the radio, Steve could see him slowly moving toward where the boat had come to rest. Fortunately, the boat had stopped a good hundred feet from shore, far enough away that the guard was having trouble, even with his flashlight, to make out what was going on or who might have been onboard. While the guard's attention was focused on the water, Steve had already walked toward the power plant, where he knew the guard had left his golf cart. He could have just taken the key, but that would not have been nearly as much fun as what he actually decided to do. He looped one end of the dock line around the back axle of the cart, pulled it through the line's swaged loop, and tightened it snugly. The other end of the twenty-five-foot line he tied securely around the trunk of a stout palm.

With that part of his plan in place, he moved about fifty yards down the cart path and pulled out the roll of heavy fishing leader. He tied one end of the line around the trunk of a palm, just a little below knee level. He stretched the line across the path, pulling it as tightly as he could, wrapped it around another palm, and tied it off. He then dropped back another twenty feet along the path and repeated the process. When he was through, he hid behind a trunk and took a minute to see what the guard was up to.

He could see him still standing near the shore, watching the boat and talking on the radio. Apparently, whoever he was talking with had concluded that the boat must have been a ruse, because Steve heard him sign off, and then saw him walking back toward the cart. He was using his flashlight, which worried Steve a little. If the guard saw the dock line, then Steve knew that he was going to have to improvise. Fortunately, however, the guard missed the line. At that moment, Steve was glad that Terry had not bleached his boat's lines in a while. He remembered seeing mold and mildew on the lines, noting that it had discolored them significantly, which, in the process, had created a perfect camouflage for the dark night.

The guard hopped into the cart, turned the key to the "on" position, turned on the cart's lights, and backed up a few feet while turning to get the cart pointed back toward the center of the island. Steve chuckled to himself as he saw this go down, knowing that the greater distance the guard had created by backing up a few feet, meant that the cart would be going even faster when it finally reached the end (so to speak) of its rope. And he was even happier when, after he had slapped the transmission into forward, the guard smashed the cart's gas pedal to the floor. Electric motors, with which this cart was equipped, produce their maximum torque almost instantly. Consequently, the cart had reached its maximum theoretical velocity by the time the dock line snapped taught. Fifteen miles per hour might not sound like all that much, but the forces involved when that amount of momentum comes to an instantaneous stop are actually quite impressive. In this case, it was impressive enough to rip the back axle assembly completely out from underneath the cart's chassis—and impressive enough to rapidly propel the guard's unprotected nose into the cart's hard plastic steering wheel. Unfortunately for the guard, this unexpected contact resulted in said nose becoming significantly flatter and shorter.

Steve observed that it took a few seconds for the guard to gather his wits—or, perhaps, to wake up. Steve wasn't sure which. However, he could tell when it actually happened because he then heard a torrent of what he assumed were curse words. Actually, even though they were in German, it didn't take much imagination on Steve's part to understand what was being said. *Goddamn*, *asshole*, and *shit* were all unmistakable parts of the monologue.

The guard's next actions were just what Steve had anticipated. He crawled out, took a quick look at the rear of the cart, and then, realizing what had happened, started to run down the path toward the safety of his associates. But he didn't get that far. The transparent fluorocarbon leader would have been hard enough to see even in broad daylight; at night, it was impossible. The guard's legs hit it full stride, which sent him cartwheeling. The end result was that his already damaged face impacted the ragged, shell-infused asphalt aggregate of the cart path with a considerable amount of force. That blow was not actually enough to knock him out; however, the next one did.

Steve was standing behind a palm a few feet from where he had secured the trip line. Consequently, when the guard fell, his head landed almost exactly opposite Steve's feet. All Steve had to do was move the heavy metal head of his cane toward the guard's cranium and, with a simple crack of his wrist, deliver enough force against the guard's bald spot to send him into a short period of dreamless sleep. This gave Steve plenty of time to secure the guard's arms, legs, and mouth with several wraps of duct tape.

Once that job was completed, Steve thought long and hard about taking the guard's guns. However, after consideration, he decided to not do that, reasoning that once guns were involved, the odds for something really bad happening would become much, much higher. Instead, he took the pistol from the guard's belt and the long gun from the cart and hid them behind the power plant. Then he started to walk toward the cottages, taking care to stay off the cart path, and, as much as possible, to stay hidden in the moon shadows created by the palms. He had not heard anything from Terry's end of the island. He assumed that to be a good thing.

Chapter Forty

Terry's initial stop had been at the stern of the guard boat, where its twin Yamaha 250s hung, waiting to be called into service. He did what needed to be done there and then swam slowly down the shore toward where he could see a guard standing next to the embers of the fire set with the first explosion. As he swam, he couldn't help but grin, thinking about how he was trying to swim quietly, with just as much stealth, and producing just as few ripples, as did the alligators he so often hunted. He hoped he had better luck than those gators.

When he'd swum a couple hundred feet, he found what he'd been looking for: a place where he could slip out of the water, unseen by the guard. At this spot, the outline of the shore was broken by a drainage ditch. He could see that the ditch ran across the island and that, a hundred feet or so inland, it was spanned by a small bridge. The slope alongside the bridge looked like a perfect place to slither out of the water, allowing him, once he was ashore, to lie prone and scan the scene with only the top of his head exposed. *Those gators know what they are doing.*

The next part of the plan was taken straight from hog hunting 101. All he had to do was place a noose someplace where the guard was sure to step and then, once a foot was inside, snatch the rope tight, pull the guard's feet out from under him, and, finally, tie him up. Terry considered for a moment where to place the loop. He thought about spreading it out on the cart path between the cart and where the guard was standing. However, he eventually concluded that there was too much risk of being seen doing that. Instead, he decided to just put it on the floor of the cart itself, right where the guard would have to step to get onboard. It was also convenient that the cart itself provided a little shadow on the side away from the dying fire. Now, all Terry had to do was to wait for the quarry to come back to the cart.

Generally, when hunting, Terry was as patient as Job. He understood full well that usually, the best thing for him to do was to stay perfectly quiet and simply wait for the animal he was hunting to wander at his own pace into his trap. But tonight, Terry was not patient. He was too worried about Jim to be patient. Therefore, he decided to do what he could to hurry the guard along.

Terry had hunted all of his life, but whereas most hunters were content to pursue the species that the government had specified as being expendable—deer, turkey, and quail—that was far too tame for Terry's taste. He'd be the first to admit that turkeys were clever enough to provide a real challenge for any hunter; however, the challenge of outsmarting a bird with a peanut-sized brain was just not enough for him. For him, it wasn't enough to simply outsmart the prey anyway. For some reason, that just didn't really seem to be a fair enough proposition from a sporting sense. The only animals he truly enjoyed pursuing were those creatures that were able to fight back, and which, if successful in the fight, could retaliate in a potentially deadly manner. At the top of his list of favorites were rattlesnakes, wild hogs, and alligators. Over the years he had developed a long list of skills and tricks that he could employ to give him the upper hand when tracking these three targets down. When dealing with alligators, one of his favorite tricks was to imitate the sound of a bull gator serenading a female. When done properly and with enough enthusiasm, this call was enough to cause any bull gator within hearing distance to react with nothing less than rage to what he perceived as a rival trespassing on his harem. The gator would usually lose little time in coming toward the sound of the call, ready to drive off the interloper. And tonight, that was the sound Terry chose to use to get the guard's attention. He understood that there was some risk that he might actually call up a big gator, but he believed that he would be able to spook the guard into getting into the cart to leave the scene long before any bull gator would actually arrive to investigate.

A gator's call is often described as a series of deep, rumbling, grunting sounds. And it's all of those things—but it's other things, too. Some of the grunts have to taper into a high-pitched squeal, and the cadence in which all this is delivered is important. However, the subtleties of the technique were probably lost on the guard, who likely hailed from a suburb somewhere outside of Berlin. A couple of repetitions, the second delivered closer to the guard than the first, were all it took for the German to make an impassioned call on the radio. Terry could tell that he was ready to get back to the security of the guardhouse with its sheltering bright lights. As he headed toward the cart Terry was already alongside, lying quietly in the darkness, his hand grasping the loose end of the noose into which the guard would soon step.

The guard sat on the seat and swung both feet onboard the cart, placing both squarely in the middle of the loop. He reached to turn on the cart's key, but before his hand was even halfway there, Terry pulled the loop tight and yanked the guard off the cart and onto the ground. The German had automatically started to reach for his pistol, but the sharp clunk of the aluminum shark bat against his skull quickly changed his mind about that option. Or about any other option, as far as that goes. He was out cold. Terry finished the job using several two-foot long zip ties, neatly but tightly securing the guard's wrists to his ankles. It really wasn't all that different from how he "hog-tied" the boars and sows he took in the Central Florida woods. He knew this guard wasn't going to go anywhere.

With that task out of the way, he headed toward the center of the island, a skilled hunter in search of his next quarry.

Chapter Forty-One

Both Steve and Terry were working their way quietly and carefully toward the center of the island when they felt their cell phones vibrate. Ordinarily, they might have ignored the signal until a more convenient time, but they both knew that tonight was not ordinary. Sheltering the phones to prevent light from seeping out, they read:

"They're moving Jim to boat!"

Steve was working along the backside of the island, about halfway between the generator, the lab, and the cottages. He was at least a quarter of a mile away from the boat dock on the northwestern shore. In the dark, it would take him a while to cover that much ground. Still, he headed in that direction.

Terry had worked his way around the front side of the main house, noticing as he did so that there were only a couple of lights turned on. He'd taken a couple of minutes to peer into as many windows as he could but saw no signs of anyone in the building. So he'd moved onto toward the pool area. He was there, studying the gorilla and his cage, when the text came in. He was much closer to the boat dock than Steve was, but by the time he'd worked his way between the house and the lab to where he could see the boat, it was too late to help Jim. He saw two guards quickly pushing and pulling what looked to be a hospital gurney down the dock. In the dark he thought he could make out that there was a human form on top of that cart. He could only watch as the guards positioned the gurney parallel with the gunwale of the boat and look on as they each lifted one end of the limp figure and dropped it into the boat. From the *thunk* Terry heard when the figure landed on the deck of the boat, he knew that the guards had not been especially worried about the health of their passenger. He watched as one of the guards jumped into the boat and positioned himself behind the controls. Terry grinned when he heard the guard fire-up the two big engines.

The guard remaining on the dock untied the lines and threw them into the boat. Then, using his foot, he shoved the bow of the big inflatable away from the dock and gave a small wave to the driver. He could hear them say something to each other in German, and then they both laughed. Terry didn't think that sounded good for Jim. But then again, he knew that they wouldn't be taking Jim as far away as they may have planned.

Terry could see the guard piloting the boat reach down toward the combined throttle and transmission control. He was apparently in a hurry, not wanting to spend time idling away from the dock. Instead, he leaned forward and engaged the controls to generate full power. Terry heard the twin motors rev and watched as the back of the boat squatted into the water as the props took their bites. The boat started to leap onto a plane, but before that could completely happen, both engines issued a funny noise, sounding almost as if they were being strangled, and then they both went silent. The boat by this time had moved at least fifty feet away from the dock, and Terry could tell that it had enough momentum to drift at least twice that far out into the bay before it would finally come to a stop. He didn't know if the guard could swim or not; regardless, he would be unable to interfere onshore for a while. And as far as Jim was concerned, although Terry couldn't help him right then, at least he knew where he was. He just hoped that the guard wouldn't try to throw him overboard. There was nothing Terry could do to prevent that from happening. However, he knew that if the guard was silly enough to drown Jim, there was plenty that Terry would do to him later. At the moment his attention was focused on the other guard.

He saw him throw both hands up in the air, displaying the universal sign that asks, "What the fuck?" Then he heard them yell something to each other. The guard on the dock appeared to have more seniority as he was the one giving the orders. Terry sensed that he told the guard on the boat to do something to fix the engines, and then he turned and walked up the pathway between the lab and house. Terry was relieved to see the guy on the boat head toward the engines. He was also relieved to see the other guard walking directly toward where he was hiding.

The guy was in a hurry to get to where he was going and obviously knew the ground well; even in the dark, he was taking long strides. He also was clearly upset; Terry could hear him muttering to himself in German. He was muttering what, to Terry, sounded like the same phrases that Steve had overheard a few minutes earlier. As the guard came nearer, Terry could see more than just the silhouette that he had been able to make out from a distance. The guy was about six feet tall and extremely well-built. His shoulders were broad, and the arms swinging with purpose below them were well-muscled. His upper chest had obviously benefited from hard hours in a gym. Then it quickly tapered, with absolutely no sign of flab or a gut, to a narrow, well-defined waist. Terry could tell that this was not a guy you'd want to go one-on-one with in a fair fight. That is why there was absolutely nothing fair about how Terry whacked him with the shark bat as he came by the banyan behind which Terry was hiding.

Again, the familiar *thunk* emanated from a blow that would have knocked most people senseless. However, this time the guard, rather than falling as Terry expected, only stumbled before turning quickly to face the direction from which the blow had come. Terry then heard him roar, his anger, fear, and adrenalin combining to transform the human into something that more closely resembled a beast. Terry could see the guard's eyes scanning, looking for who had attacked him, and then, as soon as he locked onto Terry's face, he charged. The guard clearly still had his wits. He held his head upright so that he could see who he was going to have to fight. And even though he was coming at Terry quickly, he was still well balanced, with his knees bent and his feet under him. There was no question but that this guy was a formidable foe. He had to have been half of Terry's age, well trained and in great shape. In contrast, Terry was old, a little bit arthritic, and still recovering from the recent installation of a heart stent.

Most would have assumed that Terry's odds were not that good. That's probably what the guard was thinking once he glanced at Terry's weather-creased face. But one thing Terry had going for him was experience. This was not the first time that Terry had hidden behind a tree while an enraged creature charged, trying to kill him. He'd had the same experience dozens of times. Granted, then the foe had been wild boar. However, in principal, the contest was the same.

Terry knew that what was called for was quickness and deception, along with absolute ruthlessness. To keep the guard coming toward him, he feinted to the right, like he was planning to step out in front in order to meet his attacker head on. Of course, that was what the guard was hoping for. As soon as he saw him moving out from behind the tree, he lowered his head and dove toward Terry's midsection. But Terry wasn't there as the guard flew past. Instead, now he was positioned just to the side, and slightly above, the flying strongman—positioned perfectly to bring the shark bat down on the back of the guard's head, this time with more than enough force to knock him out.

Terry had planned to hog-tie this guy just like he had done with the first guard, but when he reached for the zip ties in his back pocket, he discovered that they were no longer there. He must have dropped them on the ground. He could have just left the gym rat in the weeds; the guy was probably going to be out for some time. However, Terry didn't like to leave things to chance, and he didn't like surprises. Understanding that the guards knew where on the island to find other weapons, he wanted to make sure that this guy didn't come to and retaliate. So he grabbed him by the epaulettes on the shoulders of his uniform and dragged him. It was heavy work, but fortunately, it was only about thirty yards to the pool deck—and to the door of the gorilla's cage.

Terry had noticed earlier that that cage was secured from the outside by a heavy steel pin that dropped through a shackle that held the heavy steel door closed. The shackle and pin were protected by a heavy-duty steel mesh welded in such a way so that it was impossible to be reached from the inside. The gorilla hadn't been able to get out, and, Terry concluded, neither would the guard. And besides, Terry just kind of liked the idea of putting the guard in with the gorilla for a while. There was something about it that just appealed to his sense of justice and fair play.

Chapter Forty-Two

Steve, in the meantime, had made his way toward the shore, near where he'd seen the guard boat lying quietly in the middle of the sound. The only activity he could see was a guard trying, apparently without success, to free the prop of one of the tilted engines from a tightly wound mess of dock line. The guard was hampered by the fact that he was only barely able to reach the prop with the fingertips of one hand, the other hand being fully employed to prevent him from falling overboard. As it didn't look to Steve like there was any real risk of the guard being able to make the boat operational in the foreseeable future, he headed toward the buildings to see what he could find.

As he eased along the side of the lab, he peered into the windows that opened into the building's front room, the section where the doctor had shown Mike Collins the apparatus that transformed the cartilage from the hearts of gorillas into custom-grown, fully functioning human hearts, ready for rejection-free transplantation into the chests of critically ill patients—patients who had gladly provided the stem cells required to grow these hearts. As he looked, Steve couldn't help but notice that tonight one of the glowing beakers appeared to be empty.

He continued moving toward the rear of the lab, taking care to stay in the shadows along the building's eastern side. Once, he thought he heard a noise coming from somewhere on the other side of the building, but that was all. After that it was quiet. He was trying to decide whether to move into the light at the end of the building to test the lock on the door when he felt his cell vibrate. He pulled it from his pocket and took a look.

"WTF? Kenny."

Steve typed back, "1 guard; 1 on boat. Steve."

Just then I saw another message come in. "I got 2. Terry."

Then, "Jim? Kenny."

Terry replied, "In boat, w guard. Terry"

Quickly, Kenny responded, "Damn. Kenny."

Next, Terry asked, "Steve, w r u? Terry."

Steve replied, "E side lab. U? Steve."

To which Terry responded, "Stay. I b there. Terry."

Less than a minute later, Steve heard Terry's voice. "Steve, I'm coming in." That was followed quickly by the sight of Terry moving silently around the edge of the light.

Soon, standing next to Steve, Terry asked, "Have we got 'em all?"

"We've got all the guards," Steve said. "What about the doctor?"

"Don't know. But I didn't see him in the house," Terry replied. "Have you seen anyone else?"

"No. But I haven't really looked around that much. We need to," Steve said.

"Yep, we do," Terry responded.

But before they could say anything else, they were startled by brilliant blue strobe lights that suddenly appeared in the mouth of the bay, followed almost immediately by the piercing wails from the electronic sirens of the two Lee County Sheriff's Department patrol boats. The boats both had strong searchlights blazing as those onboard tried to make sense of what was going on about them.

Steve and Terry, as soon as they saw the blue lights, started moving toward the dock where the Zodiacs were heading. They were delighted that Mike Collins's troops were finally on scene and began waving to welcome the deputies. But that joy did not last long.

The searchlights quickly locked onto them, and as the boats neared the dock, the siren sounds were replaced by loud-speakered demands from the deputies onboard.

"You, on the shore. Place your hands on top of your heads and kneel on the ground facing us. Once you have done that, do not move, or you will be shot!"

As if to emphasize the seriousness of the instructions, one of the boats energized its siren to deliver a short blast of deafening sound. While this was happening, Steve had placed one hand over his face to try to block enough of the search lights' glare so that he could see what the deputies were doing. What he saw was not encouraging. On each boat, there were two individuals calmly pointing what looked to be automatic assault rifles directly at

Steve's and Terry's chests. Steve said to Terry, "Dude, they're serious. Do what they say."

Terry responded, "Don't have to ask twice."

Both dropped to the ground, hands on top of their heads, being very careful to stay as still as possible.

The boats quickly nosed into the dock, one on each side. The two assault rifle–carrying deputies from each boat jumped off the craft and onto the dock, taking care that the muzzles of their weapons never veered away from Steve and Terry. The deputies quickly ran off the dock and onto shore, spreading out to each side as they did so.

Once they had deployed, Mike Collins stepped onto the dock and walked slowly toward where Steve and Terry were kneeling. He stopped about five feet in front of them and said, "I am placing you under arrest for trespass, felonious assault and battery, and the destruction of property, first degree. You have the right to remain silent, and anything you say may, and will, be used against you in a court of law. You have the right to secure legal counsel. If you cannot afford to pay for such counsel, one will be provided to you. Do you understand?"

Steve exploded, "Collins, what the fuck are you doing? Have you lost your mind? These storm troopers out here have abducted Jim Story. They've got him on that fucking boat right out there, and we're sure they've hurt him pretty bad. You're arresting the wrong people. Didn't you get Kenny's call?"

"Yeah. We got it, all right. Right after we got one from Sergeant Kottmeyer, informing us that they had secured Mr. Story when they found him prowling around the island. He subsequently informed us about how you gentlemen had assaulted his staff and significantly damaged property on the island. You guys, to put it mildly, are in a heap of trouble!"

At this point Terry spoke up. "Sir, with my own eyes I saw these goons take Jim Story off the island and dump him into that boat that's floating out there in the middle of the bayou. And, when I say dump, that's what I mean. I'm sure he's injured, since Jim was unconscious before they dropped him, and he had to have fallen at least four or five feet. Someone needs to get out there and check on him before they harm him anymore, or before that guy is able to take off with him."

Something in the tone of Terry's voice must have gotten Lieutenant Collins's attention. He turned and walked away from Terry and Steve and quietly spoke into the radio handset that was clipped on his shirt. Several of the deputies ran to get back aboard one of the boats, and soon it was underway toward where the island's inflatable floated. All watched in silence as the deputies approached the boat and one of them went aboard. Seconds later Steve and Terry could overhear the deputy report back.

"Sir, there is an injured man on the deck of the boat. He's breathing, but he appears to be unconscious. There is also one of the island's guards on the boat. What would you like us to do?"

Steve and Terry could overhear Collins's response. "Secure the guard and put him on our boat. You stay onboard with the injured man. Y'all tow the boat back to the dock. I'll request a medevac."

Once he had issued those instructions, Collins turned back to Steve and Terry. "Now, why don't y'all tell me your side of the story?"

Steve started to reply, but before he could get started, he felt his cell phone vibrate. The Lieutenant heard it, too, and said, "Go ahead and answer it. It's probably your lovely wife checking up on you."

Steve looked at the text. It was from Kenny. "WTF? Kenny."

Steve typed back, "Fuzz here. U come. Steve."

We had finished, Steve looked up at Collins and said, "That was from Kenny. He's coming in. Probably will dock over on the back side of the island."

"Thank you. Any more of the 'Over the Hill Gang' out here that I should know about?" Collins asked.

"Nope," Steve responded. "Just the four of us."

"What was he doing out there?" Collins asked.

"He was just keeping an eye of things, using a night vision scope. He's the one who called you."

"Yeah. It was cute of you guys to call in once you knew Kottmeyer had already reported you. How about Kottmeyer and the rest of the guards? Where are they, and what are their conditions?"

Terry replied, "Two are tied up, one on each end of the island. Kottmeyer is taking a nap with the gorilla."

"What do you mean, taking a nap with the gorilla? Is he OK?"

"Don't know how he's doing," was the only reply he got.

"Christ, what a bunch of geriatric, imbecilic idiots I've got to deal with out here on Pine Island! For your sakes, you better pray that those guards are all OK. As soon as the boat's tied up, I'll send some guys out to bring them in. Then, hopefully, we can start to make sense of this mess y'all have created. Y'all stay where you are. Once I have my guys search you, then y'all can sit, and put your hands down. I'm going to check on Jim."

With that, he ordered the deputies to search them; and he told one deputy that when he had finished with them, he should go to the backside of the island and bring Kenny to join Steve and Terry. Then Lieutenant Collins walked over to the dock to meet the incoming boats.

As he walked away, Steve and Terry could hear him speaking into his radio microphone, apparently talking to the department's dispatcher. They couldn't hear everything he said but thought they picked up "...mess out here...need more deputies...crime scene unit, too."

Chapter Forty-Three

Once the lieutenant had walked away, Steve turned to Terry and said, "Damn. I think we're in trouble. If all they did was pick up Jim for trespassing, then we really stepped in it when we started whacking those guys and screwing around with their stuff."

Terry replied, "Maybe. Maybe not. I just hope Jim's OK."

"Yeah. Me, too. So, you put one of your guys in with the gorilla, huh?"

"Yep. The bastard pissed me off, coming after me the way he did. And besides, I don't like the idea of them keeping that monkey penned up like that. It just ain't right. That ape's got as many rights as we do. I wish I'd have gone ahead and let him out."

"I wish you had, too. That would have really given Collins something to worry about."

As they were chuckling about the gorilla they kept their eyes on the boat where Jim was. They didn't like that he was apparently still unconscious. And they were even more concerned when they heard Collins swear and saw him jump down into the boat. Then, Collins appeared to be bending over Jim and shining a small flashlight at where he was lying. Thirty seconds later, the lieutenant stood up, and they could see him talking on his radio, but they couldn't hear what he was saying. Then, after he spoke to the deputies in the boat, he stepped up onto the dock and headed their way.

"What are you stupid bastards trying to pull now?" Collins asked, once he had reached them. "I thought you told me that Jim Story was onboard that boat?"

To which Terry slowly and carefully responded, "That's exactly what I told you. I saw those Nazis wheel him out to the boat on that gurney that's still sitting there, and I saw them dump him in the boat. And I believe they would have taken him out and dumped him the gulf if I hadn't messed their boat up."

By this time the deputy who had been sent after Kenny shoved him next to Steve and Terry. When he saw Kenny, Terry said, "Kenny, you saw the guards take Jim to the boat. Tell Mike what you saw."

"That's right," Kenny replied. "Not only that, but I saw one of them hit him on the head, knock him out, and drag him into the second cottage. Then, later, I saw two of them wheel him out to the boat on a cart."

Kenny and Terry looked at Collins defiantly. They knew what they had seen.

Collins looked back at them, studying their faces. Then he said, "Y'all all come with me." He led them onto the dock where the guards' boat was secured. When they all were alongside, he shone his flashlight toward the deck of the boat and said, "Tell me, who do you see?"

Steve, Terry, and Kenny all leaned over and looked. Then, simultaneously, Kenny and Steve exclaimed, "Oh my God! It's Tommy!"

Steve quickly looked up at Collins, and said, "Mike, you know what this means, don't you? These bastards have been holding Tommy out here all this time. Once Jim stumbled on him tonight, they knew that they needed to get rid of him, so that they could claim that they were innocent and had done nothing more than detain Jim when they found him trespassing. And they'd have gotten away with it, if Terry hadn't put those dock lines on the propellers. Collins, you've been wrong about this the whole time. I'm betting these guys killed the kid that Jim and Kenny fished up—and Tommy's brother, too. Just fucking cut 'em up so they could use pieces of their hearts to grow new organs. They cut 'em up just like they were fucking cut bait and then threw their bodies into the ocean. They would have done the same thing to Tommy if we hadn't found him tonight."

Lieutenant Collins didn't respond to Steve. Instead, he looked at Kenny and said, "What was Jim doing when you saw them hit him on the head?"

"He'd just looked into the back door of the lab," Kenny responded. "But screw that. We need to find Jim. We need to go look in that second cottage, now!"

Collins nodded and turned to the deputies who were standing nearby. "Two of you stay with this boat and do what you can for Tommy. A medevac's on the way to pick him up. When it gets here, you know what to do. The rest of you, come with me." He looked at Steve, Terry, and Kenny and added, "Y'all, too."

Kenny led the way, with Collins close behind. The rest were trying to keep up. In no time they were standing outside the cottage's front door. It was padlocked with high-quality German steel. The deputies were getting ready to try to shoot it off, in tested television fashion, when Kenny said, "Wait. I think Jim was able to see in the back door. Maybe it's easier to get in around there."

Quickly the group reassembled at the rear of the building. The door was locked from the inside, but just as Kenny had suggested, everything looked less substantial. In no time, three deputies, along with Steve and Terry, were able to break the door open.

Inside, they found me sitting in a corner of the room, my feet and ankles bound together and my mouth covered with duct tape. As soon as I was free, I said, "What did they do with Tommy? You've got to find him!"

Mike Collins responded, "Don't worry. We've got Tommy. He's going to be OK. What about you? Are you OK?"

"Yeah. I'm just pissed off that I let those bastards jump me. And my head hurts a little. But otherwise, I'm just fine. Did you get the doctor?"

Everyone looked at me stupidly. Finally, Collins asked, "What about the doctor? We haven't seen him. Is he here?"

"He's in the back of the lab building," I told them. "It's an operating room. He was cutting somebody up in there when I stuck my head in. You need to find him!"

We all raced out of the cottage and headed for the lab's back door, Collins in the lead. He didn't hesitate at all when he got there; he twisted the handle and swung open the door. However, they only took a step or two inside before they all stopped, mouths and eyes wide open.

Standing over a brightly lit body on an operating table, wearing a blood-spattered cap, gown, and mask, was Dr. Areola. He was holding what looked like surgical tools in his hands. He calmly looked at us as we came in, staring directly into Lieutenant Collins's eyes. It was almost as if he were commanding us, through nothing other than the force of his will, to come no further. We all stopped.

He said, "Please, you must not proceed into this room. If you do, there is a risk you will contaminate the atmosphere and greatly increase the risk for my patient. You must all leave now, quickly, and close the door behind you. When I am through, and when my patient is stable, I will step outside to meet with you." With that, he quietly returned to closing his patient's chest.

I didn't know if it was out of respect for the doctor or fear for the patient, but for whatever reason, Collins decided to honor the directive that Areola had given. We, of course, had no choice but to follow his lead. Quietly we filed outside and closed the door. I wasn't sure about everyone else, but personally, I did my best not to breathe anymore until I was outside. Once we had all exited, Collins sent two deputies to guard the front door. The rest of us milled around outside the back door.

While we were waiting, we heard a chopper approaching. A deputy helped to guide it down near the dock. None of us spoke as we watched the medics run to the boat and then, with the deputies' help, place Tommy on a backboard and lift him to the dock. We watched them go through a quick process of determining his vital signs in a calm, professional manner. I was relieved to see, as they took those readings, that there were no obvious signs of panic, no evidence of needing to hurry. I thought that was a good sign. But who knows, maybe even if Tommy had been coding or something, those guys would probably been just as calm. Soon Tommy was onboard and headed for Lee Memorial. As soon as the chopper lifted off, one of the deputies who had assisted the medics ran over to give us a report.

"They think the guy was doped or something. They said it was almost like he was in a coma. But his vitals are strong. They said that he also appeared to have some scrapes and contusions from being thrown in the boat, but they didn't think they were serious. I got the sense that they think he's going to be OK."

We all exchanged glances, nodding our heads to indicate relief. After that there was nothing to do but wait. I could tell that Collins was starting to get antsy. I suspected that he was starting to question his decision to let the Doctor have his way. We must have waited an additional five minutes before the door to the lab was finally opened by Dr. Areola. We couldn't make out his features as he was backlit by the blinding white light from the operating room. All we could see was his silhouette, surrounded by what almost looked like a halo. We knew it was just the effect of the dazzling light leaching around his outline, but still, it was eerie to observe. As we shielded our eyes from the glare, he spoke, using language that was strangely formal and somehow inappropriate for what was actually going on. It was almost as if he, in his mind, was somewhere else.

"I must apologize for my rude behavior in the operating theater. But, as I am sure you will appreciate, it is of utmost importance that the operating environment must be maintained in an absolutely sterile condition at all times. You gentlemen, I'm afraid, had not been properly sterilized in order to be granted admittance into the theater. However, in this case I doubt that any damage was done as the patient's chest cavity had, by the time of your arrival, already been closed. I must insist, however, that in the future, should you desire to observe a transplantation procedure, you must make the proper arrangements with my staff. Now, Lieutenant Collins, if you would be so kind, I would like to request you to please join me for a few moments in my laboratory. Our conversation should take, I should think, no more than a few minutes. And, lest any of you be concerned, I will give you all my word, as a gentleman, that no harm will come to Lieutenant Collins."

With those words, he stepped outside, shut the door, and turned to walk toward the front of the building. Collins shrugged his shoulders and followed. Before he went, he said to us all, "I'll be OK." Then, speaking directly to his deputies, he said, "Y'all go mop up the guards." Then he followed the doctor.

"Jeez," one of the deputies said to another. "Just when you think it can't it get any weirder out here on Pine Island."

Chapter Forty-Four

Steve and Terry told the deputies where to find the guards they had tied up. We also told them that we'd check on the one in the gorilla cage. By this time other deputies were starting to arrive, some of whom were displaying elevated levels of stress about Collins being alone with a mad doctor. However, we passed along the instructions he had given and went to check on the gorilla and the guard.

I guess I was more worried about the guard; Terry, on the other hand, seemed to be more concerned with the gorilla. Steve and Kenny both seemed to be rather ambivalent, joking, as we walked toward the cage, about which creature might have come out on top.

When we got there, I was relieved to see the cage door still locked. Then, armed with a couple of flashlights, we looked inside. I'd guess we were all concerned about what we might see. I know that I was relieved to see that Kottmeyer's eyes were wide open, but then I noticed that he wasn't moving. In fact, he looked to be almost catatonic—possibly petrified with fear. However, that was understandable, given that the gorilla was holding the guard in his lap and gently stroking Kottmeyer's head with his gigantic hand. As we watched, we saw the guard's eyes turn in our direction, silently pleading with us to rescue him.

Kenny, Steve, Terry, and I talked it over but quickly concluded that as Kottmeyer didn't appear to be in any imminent danger, and as the gorilla seemed to be very much enjoying himself, it would probably be best to leave things as they were and return to the lab.

As we walked back around the palms we could see, in the light from the bulb over the door, that Lieutenant Collins was standing outside, talking with several of his troops. As we approached we could hear him saying, "The patient, who apparently is some Spanish big shot, has just had an open heart transplant. He is obviously in very critical condition at the moment, and he cannot, under any circumstances, be moved. According to the doctor, it is imperative that he stay absolutely quiet for at least twenty-four hours, and he has to stay hooked up to all kinds of ventilators, monitors, pumps, and who knows what else until it is clear that his new heart is functioning properly. I'm going to talk with the captain about this, but it seems to me that we've got to get a cardiac team from Lee Memorial out here ASAP to take charge of this patient. In the meantime, I've got no choice but to leave him in the care of Dr. Areola. Y'all know what to do about securing the scene. I'll let you know what we're going to do about the patient as soon as we make that decision. Get the guards on the way to Fort Myers, and let me know when the tech guys arrive."

"Mike," I interrupted, "Did you get anything from Frankenstein about Tommy's brother or about the other kid?"

"No. Not yet. But he's supposed to be writing out a statement for me in there right now about what all has gone down."

"Are you just going to leave him in there by himself?" I asked.

"You got a better suggestion?"

I had to admit that I didn't. However, I did feel proud of myself by being able to remind the Lieutenant that he should also probably try to get someone out here from the zoo. At that point, Collins just rolled his eyes.

With that, Terry and Steve walked off to retrieve Terry's boat. Kenny and I went to check on the *Pulapanga*. By this time the night's blackness was beginning to transition into the gray of dawn, giving the first sign of promise that the long night was going to finally end. We climbed aboard the boat and sat for a few minutes on its gunwale, facing the east. We were both exhausted. Then, as we watched, the leaden sky gradually began to dissolve into a rose-tinted panorama. I don't know about Kenny, but I know that I was absolutely thrilled to be able to see the sun come up one more time. There had been times during the night when I didn't think I would have that opportunity.

Maybe it was because the vibes had gotten too intense. Or maybe it was something else. Regardless, I couldn't help but laugh when Kenny broke the spell by asking, "You want a beer?"

Normally, I didn't drink beer, and I was certain that I'd never drunk one at sunrise. However, I've got to admit that at that moment, the taste of that Bud Light rivaled the taste of anything I have ever put in my mouth. The second one wasn't bad, either.

Chapter Forty-Five

As we finished our breakfasts of brew, we saw Steve and Terry coming back from the other side of the island. We walked in their direction, getting to the lab's back door at about the same time.

"Everything OK on the boat?" I asked.

"Yeah. Right where I left it," Steve responded. "But, damn it, we're starting to get hungry. Did y'all have anything to eat?"

"No," I answered truthfully. "But there are some cans of Vienna sausage in the radio locker. You're welcome to those."

"Sounds good to me. Terry, you want one?" Steve asked.

"You bet," Terry replied.

"Hey, Steve," I said. "Since you're going that way, why don't you bring a couple for Kenny and me, too?"

Kenny chimed in. "And, Steve, could you bring me a beer?"

Steve just shook his head and headed for the boat. He returned shortly, bearing all the requested items plus a couple of extra beers. We were all just licking our fingers when we saw Mike Collins wave for us to join him.

When we got there, he said, "I thought you guys would like to hear this. I've got a written statement from the doctor. He admits to killing the Mermaid Guy, and Tommy's brother, too. He said he also did some guy in Spain. Apparently, he'd have Kottmeyer grab a drunk walking along Stringfellow. They didn't even know who the guys were, and they didn't care. All that the doctor wanted were their hearts so that he could use them to grow replacements for the diseased hearts of his investors. They each had put up five million dollars and borrowed that much more. In return, they got new hearts, and a sixteen and a half percent share of the rights to the process that Dr. Areola was developing. The guy in there tonight was the last of them. According to the doctor, the investors didn't have any idea about the need to murder someone in order for them to get their new hearts. They believed the story about using cartilage from gorillas all along."

"Mike, if all the investors had gotten their hearts, why were they holding Tommy?" I asked.

"They'd caught him sneaking around on the island the night after we'd last seen him and the dog. They didn't really need Tommy's heart at that moment but figured they'd keep him in inventory, so to speak. They didn't know about the dog being with Tommy, and it was able to get away. The guards took the boat out into the sound and planted the empty bottle on board to make it look like he'd fallen out."

"Is Tommy going to be all right?" I asked. "Did the doctor have anything to say about that?"

"He said that he would be fine. They'd simply hooked him up to a drip that kept him in a semi-comatose state. As soon as the drugs wear off, he'll be fine. But he won't remember anything about this."

"So where's the doctor now?" Steve asked.

"For now, until the team gets here from Lee Memorial, I need his assistance to keep the patient alive. He's monitoring his signs from a terminal in his office over at the house and periodically checking on the guy."

"You let him go back to the house?" I asked.

"Yeah. It's not like he can go anywhere. He requested to organize his papers and records about his processes. He's very concerned that once he's arrested, he won't be able to, and he wants to make sure that this information will eventually find its way into the hands of the best cardiac researchers here and in Spain. I'm not worried about him doing anything silly since I've got a deputy with him to keep an eye on what he's doing."

"Did you find all the guards? Are they OK?"

"Yeah. We found them right where you left them. They weren't going anywhere." Mike replied.

"How about the guy I left with the gorilla?" Terry asked. "Were you able to get the gorilla to let him go?"

Mike laughed and said, "The guys and the monkey had a standoff for a while, but once Kottmeyer told them where they kept the bananas, they were able to negotiate his release without too much drama."

"So what's going to happen to him?" Terry asked.

"Who? Kottmeyer?"

"I don't give a shit about him!" Terry exclaimed. "What's going to happen to the monkey?"

"The zoo's sending some guys out here to pick him up. But they didn't sound all that excited about having to do that." Mike answered.

"Collins," Terry said. "I'm going to tell you something, and I'm as serious as a heart attack when I say this. I'm not too happy about the prospect of that big guy having to go back into a cage just so snotty-nosed yard apes can point at him and call him names. You tell the zoo that I have a friend up in Central Florida who runs a wildlife sanctuary with over a thousand acres for critters to just roam around in. Tell the zoo to call me as soon as the ape's on the mainland. My friend and I will pick up the monkey and release him up there."

"That sounds good," Mike replied. "I'll make sure that happens."

"Now, what about us?" I asked. "You need us to hang around?"

"No. Y'all can take off. I'll make arrangements in the next day or two to get formal statements from each of you. There's no reason for you to stick around here any longer."

"All right, Mike," I said. "We'll clear out. But before we go, I want you to know that I really appreciate you getting out here as quickly as you did. You probably saved Tommy's life."

Mike looked me in the eye and said, "I doubt that. I'm pretty sure that Steve and Terry would have been able to have kept anything from happening to him."

Steve and Terry said nothing in reply.

Collins chuckled and said, "All right. Y'all get out of here."

Chapter Forty-Six

Kenny and I headed toward the *Pulapanga*. Steve and Terry walked to where Terry's boat was tied up. As soon as we were underway, idling through the no wake zone, I called Jill on the cell. As I did, I noticed Kenny take out his phone, too.

Jill answered on the first ring. Before I could even say hello, she asked, "You alive?"

"Yeah. I'm fine. Wanted to let you know that we're all OK and on our way home."

"We've all been worried to death about y'all," Jill said.

"Who's we?" I asked.

"Katie, Patty, Roxie, Georgia, Carolyn, Janice, and Gigi have been here with me all night. Kenny kept us up to date for a while, texting us what was going on. But we hadn't heard anything from him since about three o'clock."

"Yeah. That's probably about when I got hit on the head," I replied.

"Oh my God! Are you OK?" Jill asked.

"Yeah, I'm good. We're all good. Who's Janice? And, who's Gi Gi?"

"Janice is the lady Roxie and Georgia introduced Kenny to. Gi Gi is her sister. I like them both. And I think Kenny does, too. In fact, I think he just called Janice," Jill said.

"Yep. He's on the phone. We're on the way. Be there soon. Love you, baby."

"Love you, too. Be careful. Bye."

We arrived at my dock in a little less than an hour. As we walked toward the house, we couldn't help but notice a number of cars in the driveway and the sound of voices spilling out of the open French doors on the house's main level. It was the sound of a party, a sound not at all unusual for Saint James City. However, the sounds of a party at seven o'clock in the morning were, admittedly, not all that common.

As we walked up the stairs, we were enticed by the magic smell of fried bacon, and when we opened the door, the first thing we saw was a kitchen full of breakfast foods. Eggs, bacon, sausage, sliced tomatoes, cheese toast, and biscuits and gravy were just the first things we saw. On another countertop, Delmar O'Riley was supervising the preparation of his specialty, the island's best Bloody Marys. Delmar, genuinely one of the island's nicest people, looked right at home in the kitchen. Then again, he should have, considering that Jill and I had purchased our house a few years earlier from him and his lovely, gracious wife, Carolyn. By this time they were two of our very best friends. That's just the way things tended to happen on Pine Island.

And the morning's Bloody Mary breakfast bash had apparently happened the way parties also tended to just happen on Pine Island. No sooner had the news that we had all survived spread on the island's grapevine than a welcome home party was organized. "Organized" is probably too strong a word to use to describe the process. Here on the island, these things just tended to develop—it was almost as if they erupted spontaneously. Everyone volunteered to bring a dish along with a bottle of wine or liquor. Georgia's husband brought a cooler of ice from his commercial-sized icemaker, along with a large sack of delicious ripe tomatoes from his farm in the Glades. Georgia whipped up a wonderful egg casserole. Roxie brought a couple dozen organic eggs that she had just purchased the day before when she'd had her hair done. (The island's favorite hairstylist also had a sizable chicken coop in her backyard.) Delmar supplied the tomato juice. He was reported to buy it by the case at the Sam's Club in the Cape. On and on, everyone had contributed something. And, par for the course, the party was happening.

As soon as we had Bloody Marys in our hands, we looked around and noticed Steve and Terry standing on the porch, surrounded by ladies listening intently as they described their roles in the night's activities. I couldn't help but also notice the dog Dixie standing alongside, happily wagging her tail, as she listened to their stories. I sensed that the dog understood what the morning's festivities were about.

I noticed also that it only took a matter of seconds before Kenny and Janice had found each other. I smiled as I saw them hold hands and move toward a quiet corner of the room, gazing intently into each other's eyes as they did so.

However, look as I might, I couldn't find Jill. Everyone was trying to talk to me, but I couldn't stop to do that until I had found her. Finally, I saw her coming up the stairs from the lower level, a case of beer in one hand and a bottle of vodka in the other. As soon as we saw each other we made a beeline for each other, our bodies melting together as our lips touched. I hugged her as tightly as I could, not even giving her a chance to put down the beer and the booze. For that moment, it wasn't as if time stood still; it was more like it simply had ceased to exist. So I don't know how long we actually stood there like that. However, eventually, we could no longer ignore the fact that we were surrounded by half the town's citizens who were looking at us, fondly and silently. The spell was finally broken when someone yelled, "Get a room!" That did it. From then on, it was party time. Steve, Terry, Kenny, and I must have each told our stories at least a dozen times. And every time we did, someone would slap us on the back and hand us another drink.

I guess it must have been close to noon before everyone left. And not long after that, I was sound asleep. I didn't even make it as far as the bedroom; instead, I made the tactical error of sitting down to rest for what I thought would only be a minute or two on the comfortable, cushioned wicker couch on the screened porch overlooking the canal. The sun had already started to set when I finally came to, startled, I think, by the sound of a jumping mullet.

Jill was inside, watching television, when I staggered in, still rubbing my eyes to wake up.

"Did you have a nice nap?" she asked.

"Yeah. I guess I must have," I replied. I walked over to give her a kiss.

She reciprocated, but in a somewhat less enthusiastic manner than I had anticipated. "What's the matter?" I asked.

"Nothing that you taking a good shower, brushing your teeth, and putting on some fresh clothes, won't cure."

"That bad, huh?"

"Let's just say that I've smelled crab traps that smell better than you. You go get cleaned up, and then I thought we might go down to Red's for dinner. You in the mood for a good steak?" she asked.

"Fantastic! I won't be long."

Chapter Forty-Seven

We had a great dinner. Then, back at home, we had an even better evening, gladly shedding our clothes as we climbed the stairs toward the familiar sanctuary of our queen-sized bed. There's nothing like a brush with eternity to remind you how much being with the person you love means to you. It was a night to cherish.

The next morning brought news. The first surprise came as we flipped on the morning's local news cast and learned that Dr. Areola had died on Little Bokeelia Island. The reporter, standing in the bright morning sun in front of the Burgess Manor, was doing her best to summarize what had taken place on the island. She had most of the story right. I was impressed that she had been able to manage that, considering I knew that much of what had taken place there had simply been almost unbelievable. However, there was no doubting her report that the doctor had taken his own life in the manor the previous morning. While his picture was being shown on the screen, we heard her say that he had apparently managed to take his own life by swallowing some pills, even though he was being guarded at the time by a Lee County sheriff's deputy. The reporter, doing her best to dramatize the story by hinting at the possibility of foul play on the part of the sheriff's department, promised that the station would follow up with additional details as soon as they became available. Jeez. I felt bad for Mike Collins. I knew that he was going to have some explaining to do.

The second surprise came via a phone call. Jill, recognizing Roxie's number on the caller ID, picked up the phone. I could tell from the look on her face, and from the various "ooh," "ah," and "isn't that sweet" comments she kept interjecting, that Roxie had some especially good news to share.

Once she hung up, I looked at her. She was simply beaming with happiness. I laughed and asked, "OK, what's up?"

"Oh," she said. "It's so sweet! I'm so happy for them."

I knew she couldn't help herself. She was, in fact, so happy that she was having trouble actually remembering to tell me what it was that she was so happy about. I let her enjoy herself for a minute or so before finally turning toward her and holding up both palms to give the universal sign of asking "What in the heck are you talking about?"

"Oh. It's so sweet! I'm so happy for them," was all that I got in reply. I knew that a stronger intervention was going to be necessary.

"Jill," I asked directly, "who are you so happy for?"

"Oh! It's so sweet," she began. For a moment I thought my intervention had failed, but then she finally spilled the beans. "Kenny and Janice are going to get married! He asked her last night. They're going to get married this weekend. Roxie is going to perform the ceremony."

I stared at her with my mouth hanging open. I knew that Kenny was in trouble when he kept describing Janice as "cute," but I hadn't expected this. At least, I had not expected it this quickly. However, I guess the encounter with eternity had affected them as well. I was truly delighted for them, as I told Jill once I had recovered my ability to speak.

"Wow! That's really great. They are such a...." I hesitated to use the word, but finally I couldn't help myself. "They are such a cute couple."

Jill replied, "Isn't that the truth? They are so cute together, and they look so happy together. Did you see, yesterday morning, how they couldn't take their eyes off of each other?"

"Now that you mention it, yes," I replied. "Did I hear you right when you said that Roxie is going to perform the ceremony? Is she a JP or something?"

"She's a notary public. Here in Florida, they can perform marriage ceremonies. In fact, she's performed dozens of them. Once, in a prior life, she owned a crewed charter yacht, and she used to marry people on her boat all the time."

"Cool!" I said.

The third surprise of the day came later that afternoon. Jill and I were in our bathing suits, sitting beside the pool and working on our tans, when we heard a car pull into the driveway. I got up to see who it was and walked out the screen door toward the front of the house. A moment later I came back into the pool cage, bringing a guest with me. "Jill," I said. "Look who's come to visit."

"Tommy!" she screamed. "How are you?" But before he could answer, she had leaped out of her lounge chair and was giving him a big hug.

"Jill, stop!" I exclaimed. "Tommy's still recovering. He doesn't have his strength back yet. Tommy, you sit down right here," I directed, pointing him toward a nearby wicker chair.

"Jill, don't you listen to that old fool," Tommy replied. "You can hug me as long as you want to. That's the best medicine that I've had since I woke up."

She hugged him again and gave him a kiss on the cheek. He looked at me and smiled before turning back to Jill and saying, "Why don't you hug me just one more time?" She did, and then, finally, he sat down.

Almost before he had finished sitting, we were both asking him, "How do you feel?"

He replied, "It just feels great to be alive! But I really am weak as hell. You'd think I'd be all rested up after lying in bed for so long, but I guess that must really take it out of you. In fact, they didn't want to let me out of the hospital, so I just checked myself out. They weren't too happy about that, but I told them that the best medicine for me would be to get back out here on the island as soon as I could. And see, I was right. None of those nurses were hugging and kissing me, I can tell you that. Jill has made me feel better already. The other reason I had to get out of there was so I could come and thank Jim for what he did. As I understand it, if it hadn't been for you, I'd still be lying there in that bed. Or somewhere worse. Jim, I want you to know that I appreciate what you did."

"Tommy, I'm glad that I could help," I replied. "But I'm sorry about your brother."

"Yeah. Me, too. But from what Mike Collins told me, there wasn't anything that we could have done. He said that my brother was dead before we even knew he was missing. Now, all I've got left to remember him by is Dixie. I understand that she's been staying with one of your friends in Bokeelia."

"Yep. Terry's got her. I'll give you his address and call him to tell you you're on the way to get her. He'll be happy for Dixie to go back to where she belongs."

"Thanks, Jim. Well, I guess I'll head on up there to pick him up."

"Sounds good," I said.

Tommy got up and started to head toward the door, but Jill stopped him by asking, "Tommy, have you heard about Kenny and Janice? They're going to get married!"

Tommy turned toward Jill, and I could see a smile on his face as he said, "Kenny? I never thought I'd see the day. That is so great. When are they going to tie the knot?"

"This Saturday afternoon," Jill responded.

"That is wonderful. That gives me something to think about. You think they'd like to have a party or something this week, to celebrate?"

"It sounds like a good idea to me," Jill said.

"I'll be in touch." Tommy walked slowly toward his car, talking quietly into his cell phone as he went.

Chapter Forty-Eight

It was six o'clock on Friday night. The tour bus pulled into the shell-covered parking lot next to Froggy's and parked. The bar was packed. It looked like everyone in town was there. However, fifteen minutes later, almost everyone who had been inside was loading onto the bus. It was time for a party. *Look out, Fort Myers! The citizens of Saint James City are coming to see you.*

Once he had heard the news about Kenny and Janice's pending nuptials, Tommy had made plans for a special way to thank the whole town for what they had done to help him. He had chartered the bus and rented the top floor of "The Firestone," downtown Fort Myers' premier party spot, for the evening. The top floor was an open-air cocktail space that overlooked the Caloosahatchee River. It was truly a spectacular place to hold a celebration.

And tonight, there was a lot to celebrate. Not only had Tommy been rescued and Kenny and Janice decided to get married. Tonight, the town was in a happy mood—a mood that became even brighter when the passengers on the bus learned that Tommy had had the foresight to stock the bus with an ample supply of both beer and liquor. The bus was rocking even before it rolled through Matlacha and off the island.

Tonight there was indeed a lot to celebrate. Because tonight, it seemed, life in Saint James City had finally returned to normal.

ABOUT THE AUTHOR

Mitch Grant, seventh-generation Floridian, is a retired banker, racecar driver, and aspiring buccaneer. As a young man, when not attending school, he worked his family's groves and ranches and spent summers in the swamps of Gulf Hammock, learning boating, fishing, and other critical Cracker skills. After graduating from Stetson University, he served in the US Army as a field artilleryman. The GI Bill provided the means to further his education, and he earned an MBA from the University of South Florida. This degree opened the door to a thirty-five year career in the commercial banking industry, where he helped to lead banks in Florida, Georgia, and Alabama. When not working, he pursued his passion for sports car automobile racing, becoming one of the nation's most experienced and best-known amateur drivers. Upon retirement from the banking industry, he and his wife, Sherry, moved to Saint James City, Florida, a quiet fishing village, where he pursued another dream: writing mystery fiction. His writing is inspired by, and modeled after, that of his literary hero and island neighbor, Randy Wayne White. Now, when not writing or fishing, he is helping to educate his four grandchildren in the ways of Southwest Florida's legendary pirates.